The Hanged Man

The Hanged Man

Don Bapst

EDITIONS

Cover design by Terry Gallagher/Doowah Design.
Photograph of Don Bapst by Rick Aguilar.
Printed and bound in Canada by Hignell Printing.

Acknowledgements
To the staff of the historic homes and museums of New York, to the generous people of Burkina Faso, and to the creators of original Tarot cards, whoever and wherever they may have been. Also to Lisa Wallace for her rigorous edits, to Doug Whiteway for first believing in the story, to Vanessa Mancini for creating a haunting video trailer, and to Karen Haughian for helping me take the novel to another level.

We acknowledge the support of The Canada Council for the Arts and the Manitoba Arts Council for our publishing program.

Library and Archives Canada Cataloguing in Publication

Bapst, Don
    The hanged man / Don Bapst.

ISBN 978-1-897109-49-6

    I. Title.

PS3602.A68H36 2010   813'.6   C2010-905618-3

Signature Editions, P.O. Box 206, RPO Corydon
Winnipeg, Manitoba, R3M 3S7
www.signature-editions.com

To Mom and Dad
for letting me choose what to believe

Chapter One

THE PAGE OF STAVES

A unique individual, a nonconformist. Independent yet consistent innovator or inventor. A wild card. Loyal friend or a stranger with good intentions. A bearer of good news.

Beneath the blond curls, his young face is sinister. His cheeks, of course, are rosy, his lips the usual Renaissance petals. Still, the eyebrows are black and arched, the eyes dark and deep. He looks up at something — no, rather someone — as if from the depths of a city evacuated in anticipation of destruction. He's weighed down by a needlessly plush velvet robe, from which his thin legs poke out like a clapper from a bell. In his right hand he holds a stave almost as long as his body — each end capped with an elaborate golden ornament. He stands on a weathered landscape — once vibrant green — his pose so calculated it would seem he is conscious that he is a symbol. But of what and to whom? His stern stance, unflinching on a background etched in gold and bordered by lapis lazuli, provides no clues about his purpose or intentions.

October 15, 1999, 1 a.m.

I have received many signs over the years, but nothing like what the cards sent me today. Their message came like a kiss from the other side of time, and it came to me in the form of a small ocher smudge.

I begin my journal confident this new revelation is the key to my destiny. Within these pages, I will trace every step in uncovering the true story of the ancient Tarot — every step of my journey along the way. Each entry will begin as this one does, with a single card drawn by me from the deck (or sent from the deck to me), setting the tone for all the events to follow.

Instead of "reading" the cards, I will study their images for clues. Now that I know their answers may lie in the intricacies of their physical construction as well as in their divinatory meanings, I must recognize their appearance, their texture, their physical *presence*.

It all happened this morning in an icily quiet research room in the Pierpont Morgan Library. For months I've waited for permission to view the original Visconti-Sforza deck — those exquisitely gilded paper rectangles commissioned by Italian nobles and handcrafted by court artists in the 15th century. Of the original 76 or 78 cards, about half are now stored in this jewel box of a library tucked away in midtown Manhattan, with the remaining cards housed in various collections in Bergamo, Italy.

To think I was finally seeing the 500-year-old cards that had inspired the old deck of playing cards I'd grown up with! How I'd loved those fragile antiques my great-grandfather had passed on for generations, discovering them at age five while snooping through my mother's secret drawer. I would take them out of the extravagant silk scarf Mom had wrapped them in to search for answers to my questions. "What will I be when I grow up?" and "Who will I marry?"

But though they were grounded in our own family history, these old playing cards held few of the images from the much older Tarot deck, so their answers remained forever numerical (8 of clubs, 4 of hearts…) and distant. In fact, it wasn't till I was a teenager that I discovered Crowley's and other decks and began really reading the cards…

Still, Visconti-Sforza, though missing a few cards, was one of the oldest surviving decks on the planet, and I was dying to see as much of it as I could. After months of waiting, my petition to the library was finally acknowledged and I was granted a private viewing based on my status as a graduate student in art history. I would be allowed to select four of the cards in the collection and view them for thirty minutes in the company of a librarian who would display each card through a protective sleeve using gloved hands.

I resisted the temptation to request only cards from the Major Arcana, the twenty-two most colorful cards in the deck. Known merely as "trump" cards by art historians who usually think of the Tarot as nothing but a nobleman's parlor game (even though the cards are revered as oracles by those who know how to use them to read into another dimension), the Major Arcana contains the Tarot's most powerful and revelatory symbols.

I asked to see The Wheel of Fortune, symbol of my search for meaning in the cards, and The Fool, image of a man bravely embarking on such a quest.

For a completely rounded perspective, I also needed to see one of the court cards, those Renaissance ancestors of our modern playing cards: kings, queens, knights, and pages (the latter two having merged into the jacks of today), and one of the pips: the cups, swords, staves, and coins that have been transformed over time into hearts, spades, clubs, and diamonds.

Just over a year ago, I knew nothing of changes to these cards over the centuries, so I suppose that studying them as an academic has paid off... Lately, though, I haven't been able to approach a reading with the same degree of awe as before. The "unknown" the Tarot once evoked for me has become more and more tangible, somehow, now that the cards have become forever fixed in my mind to dates and events in history.

Until today.

So, in addition to the two Major Arcana cards, I chose to see the Eight of Coins and the Page of Staves, the former because of the elegant symmetry of its eight golden circles — like four sets of infinity symbols or a cluster of blinding suns — the latter because it is always the card in which I most see myself, especially now that I'm open to these answers...

The librarians at the Morgan Library are fastidious, to say the least. They are working to preserve one of the world's greatest collections of antiquities, and they don't take their task lightly. They don't need hair pinned up in buns or horn-rimmed glasses to convey their authority. They needn't look up at the building's richly painted ceilings or thumb through the jaw-dropping list of precious items contained with its walls. They simply *know everything*.

They make their presence hardly known. In fact, I would scarcely be able to describe the librarian who guided me through the four cards I had selected. I remember only the quiet "whoosh" of the protective box as it slid across the table towards me in her gloved hands. I was asked to merely observe the antiquities as she placed each protected rectangle in front of me — never touching, never talking. Just seeing, listening, sensing.

500 years.

These cards had been held in the hands of the Italians who had ordered them created. Used for what purpose? To play games, as jaded historians would have everyone believe? I couldn't believe that such beauty — each card a hand-painted treasure of Renaissance art! — could only exist to kill time in some overstuffed castle. I had to prove that these cards weren't simply a European spin on the ancient Chinese game of "money cards," but a sacred tool of the ancient Egyptians brought to Europe by nomadic Arabs and Romani gypsies — a connection many occultists swore by, even if secular Tarot researchers scoffed at the notion.

For me, though, the cards were too charged with symbolism and meaning to be simply a game. Their intricate facades overwhelmed me with the fine detailing of those master craftsmen who'd created them. Each tiny brush mark, each application of pigment, a stroke of genius. For a moment, I forgot about the divinatory significance of each card and was struck merely by the beauty of the artistic technique…

And then the gloved hand unveiled the fourth card in its transparent sheath.

I had studied the reproduction of this card before viewing the original, but nothing had prepared me for the earthiness of its tone, and that smudge along the young page's profile in such a rich hue. I was reminded of Egyptian hieroglyphs and African pottery. There in the Renaissance depiction of the archetype I carry within me — this message-bearing page who has crossed centuries on his quest to enlighten others — I found the earth of Africa.

I'm not talking about a symbolic earth, but rather an actual physical quality to the pigment used to paint the card: a gritty streak of savannah sludge worn into the delicate figure as if by the cruel thumb of fate. No, it wasn't a streak, but rather more like an exposed foundation revealed through the chipped plaster of the white figure's fragile cheek.

These cards were not born in Europe.

Had I gasped out loud at my discovery, I wondered, as the librarian whisked away the final image from me? My time with the cards had come to an end. "You are lucky," she said, as she placed the page back into the box she had used to transfer it from the dark recesses of the library where it was presumably stored. "Normally this particular card is kept in Bergamo."

I was stunned. "Really? Then why is it here?"

"A wealthy collector of Tarot art was looking to verify the authenticity of a privately acquired piece…" She stopped herself as if realizing she'd revealed too much.

"But how was it that I saw it listed in the library listings?"

"It's not. We have the King of Staves." I could see she was trying to pull away, but I had so many questions.

"But I specifically requested it."

"It's possible you saw the King listed and requested this one instead by mistake. In fact, it wasn't until I pulled your request from the shelf that I realized the mix-up. A happy coincidence this one happened to be here."

There are no accidents.

"Are there other cards from Bergamo here?" I was dying to know if the Devil and Tower cards, which were supposedly missing from the 78-card deck, could actually be hidden within another collection somewhere…

"That's the only one, and it technically shouldn't be shown."

"If I…"

"We really need to keep our voices down. You can feel free to submit an additional proposal if you need to study other cards in the collection."

"I'll be back," I said. My temple was throbbing, pulsing with blood as thick as the pigments that rippled through the masterpiece I had just been shown.

I had found the beginning of my answer.

Until my teens, the cards had remained little more to me than a secret childhood friend. They were the teddy bear I stayed up with when I couldn't sleep at night. I asked them questions, but expected no real answers.

Then one night, my mother found me sprawled on the floor of the bedroom she shared with my father, the entire pack of our ancestor's yellowing playing cards spread before me. "What will become of my parents?" I asked them.

I never heard Mom enter, so I don't know if she heard my question before she slapped me across the face. Never had my mother hit me before, and the sting of the blow came not from its physical force but from the intense power of fear that had given her the momentum to deliver it.

But even more alarming was the sense of a reading gone unfinished, and a link with broken destiny. What if my mother had shaped her own fate by not allowing me to find the answer to my question? I suspected from the severity of her reaction to my innocent game that the cards were something far more powerful than I had ever imagined: a key to a door that she wanted shut forever. I never went into her things again, and never again did I see my great-grandfather's cards.

But like any teenager presented with something wondrously forbidden, I wanted nothing else from then on, and so began my love of all things divinatory. I went on to collect Ouija boards, crystal balls, and Tarot cards, studying their symbols and reading hundreds of interpretive texts to learn how to use them. I kept my growing collection a secret, though, revealing my interest in the occult only through my painting.

"If he keeps painting that crap, he's never going to get a real job," my mother would say to my father as if I wasn't within earshot. All the awards I earned, first at high school, then college art shows, were never enough to put her worries about me to rest.

"Let him be himself," Dad would argue with her, forever coming to my defense. A retired high school teacher himself, he never considered himself an intellectual, but he certainly appreciated "higher" education. Like Mom, he'd come from a working-class family on Chicago's South Side, but while he had gone through college, Mom had never finished high school. She had worked at a series of odd jobs before meeting my father in her twenties. For her, hard work equaled success. She wanted a better life for me than either of them had known, and she couldn't see how reading and writing more could give me that life. Dad had to constantly reassure her that more education was a positive step toward my success, even as he wondered about the eclectic direction I chose to take with my studies.

Not that I realized any of that as a young artist eager to share everything I had learned on my introspective journeys. I wanted only to "emerge on the scene" and show the whole world the *truth* in a way that had never been shown before.

Then one of my favorite art teachers brought me down to reality in my senior year of college with a lecture on the bleak prospects for art school grads out in the "real world." Even if I was the greatest painter and sculptor in the world, I had little chance of paying my bills that way. When I talked it over with Dad, he agreed. A Master of Fine Arts was out of the question, though I could always go for an art history degree. Not that it was a recipe for fame and wealth, but at least it would make a career as a professor possible, and, anyway, as a retired teacher, he had a few connections he could use to help me get started.

Mom frowned on the idea, but she didn't have a better plan. Anyway, nothing I seemed capable of accomplishing was going to erase her disappointment in me. If I wanted to be a teacher like Dad, then fine, but it wasn't like teachers' salaries were getting any bigger, and times were getting tough. Still, it was better than me being a completely penniless artist.

As far as I was concerned, working toward a master's in art history was about as appealing as going to business or law school, and I resisted it as best I could. But catalogs from grad programs across the country kept piling up on my desk as Dad staunchly attempted to provide me with motivation. Thumbing through them one night, I discovered a tiny program at an obscure branch of the City University of New York on the secular origins of sacred art.

The idea washed over me like the sun on a cold day, sending points of light clear down to my toes. I would turn the program inside out and write about the sacred origins in what these academics called "secular." I would study the Tarot.

Even Dad was reluctant when he heard my idea, but the program was cheap and the university was respected. We'd just keep the subject of my studies from Mom as best as we could.

Running up the stairs to the university after visiting the library today, I was more confident than ever that all the difficult choices leading up to the present were not random accidents but rather critical steps in the fulfillment of my destiny. The cards were not merely a tool for reading that destiny (as they are for so many) but an integral part of my fate.

Only a year before, after presenting my topic to my research advisor, I learned just how threatened academics would be by my vision. Dr. Carter had sent back my proposal with a single sentence, scribbled in red: "A subject perhaps better suited to the anthropology department." I cornered him in his office and begged him to reconsider.

"We'll see if you can sustain a manuscript on the topic," he sighed. "But be sure and link your research back to something pertaining to art history."

Dr. Carter was, I'd been told, a megalomaniac of epic proportions, whose work from the early 1960s on eroticism in the sacred art of the Italian Renaissance had once granted him an almost mythic status among academics. As far as anyone remembered, though, he had uncovered absolutely nothing new in the third of a century since. Like any one-hit wonder, Carter was terrified of the new, according to his detractors, and his lectures were nothing but a constant regurgitation of scholars' praise for his all-but-forgotten contributions to a highly specialized body of knowledge. I liked to think that with the right grounding, he'd have been able to push past all that, but clearly there was some kind of negative energy blocking his way.

I had tried presenting a description of my subject I thought he might find more palatable. "The Tarot (or Tarocchi, as it was called in 15th-century Italy) is like a tapestry revealed over 78 separate rectangles rather than across a single bolt of fabric. As the order of this movable, interchangeable canvas can be shifted at will, it has allowed audiences over the centuries to create an unlimited number of stories and interpretations based on the way the figures contained within the Tarocchi are juxtaposed. Plus, the unprecedented portability of these cards has allowed them to…"

"Fine, but what do you have to add to the research on these cards? They were commissioned by nobles employing the services of artisans, and they are entirely lacking in any social commentary or satire or even a sacred significance..."

"But that's not true! They are believed to have originated in ancient Egypt or even..."

"Rubbish! There's not an ounce of evidence for such speculative theories popularized by charlatan occultists. You need tangible, physical evidence of your thesis, not wishful thinking and hearsay. Now come up with a revised proposal by next month and we'll talk."

All of my conversations with Carter ended with his dismissing me in this way. I went to other professors for advice, but I discovered that while some took pity on me having to deal with Carter, no one thought any more of my subject than he did. The Tarot cards were perceived as having little more value than the most common decorative arts of the era. Not that anyone pretended the illustrations on their surfaces weren't, in many cases, spectacular, but their association with the occult in the 18th and 19th centuries seemed to taint the entire subject for most academics. It was as if they feared that merely gazing upon the cards would associate them with popular "New Age" literature — or even worse, turn them into eccentric occultists draped in purple velvet robes.

Of course the "research" on the Tarot did little to make a case for the cards' importance. The best texts were little more than catalogs, haphazardly made up of existing Tarot cards, most of which were owned by a single collector in Connecticut, who also happened to be the largest publisher of new Tarot decks in the world and a reclusive eccentric. My requests to interview him had been unceremoniously declined for months.

Other Tarot enthusiasts compiled voluminous manuscripts of every conceivable fact, theory, and opinion related to the Tarot — however vague or irrelevant — in a sometimes curious, but more often tedious and disorganized mass of unedited text. That the entire subject was avoided by most "serious" academics only made it all the more attractive to me, though much harder to justify within the university where I was pursuing my thesis.

But now I finally have the physical evidence to crack the Tarot's ancient code! As I have long known, the Middle-Age references on the surface of the Italian Tarocchi are merely a picturesque mask over multiple layers of deeper meaning. What I never suspected was that there could be actual physical layers of pigments applied in different locations, at different times. Or perhaps the gilded paints of the Renaissance had actually been applied directly on top of older cards painted in northern Africa and imported to Europe by the gypsies! That would definitely account for the astonishing ocher pigment I saw. I am quite sure now that what I saw...what I felt...was ancient.

Outside of time.

I have to find a justification for getting that card tested. Would such a thing even be possible? Surely it has been carbon dated already. But then again, maybe not. Since no one believes in the true artistic significance of the cards, maybe they've only been given a cursory examination, then cataloged and shelved for lack of interest.

Until now.

Someone else, it seemed, had seen something important in this card, something important enough to fly it in from Italy. Surely that wasn't an accident.

Damn it. I hadn't asked the librarian when the card would be sent back to Bergamo or how I might go about getting permission to do a more in-depth investigation. I'm sure I'll need to speak with a lab technician at the library. But first, I'll need someone at the university to back me about the plausibility of my theory.

The more I think of it, the more my mind races. And already the image of the card I saw only this morning is becoming fuzzy. If only I had studied it more carefully. Why had I allowed her to rush me? I have to get back in there.

It was too late to make anything else happen today. By the time I reached campus, everyone had already left. I would have to wait till Monday. I strode past the classrooms with their clumsy metal desks, my footsteps echoing in the empty hallways. Most people never notice this quiet little branch of the City University of New York, which is tucked away on a leafy street in the forties, overshadowed by the boxier buildings that surround it. It had formerly been a psychiatric care center at a time when shock treatments were more popular than communication, and I often imagine the suffering former residents must have undergone in the building's austere rooms and corridors. Thankfully, there are no photos to reference that time, and the energies of the people who lived through it seem to have dissipated.

Today, as I passed the massive oak doors at the entrance, I ran into Brad on his way into the building, a thick stack of books under a bony arm. "Glen, I'm really onto something, I think. I've just examined the earliest research on the removal of varnish during the Sistine Chapel restoration. It's totally flawed! This is going to be huge." His eyes were wild, his hair mussed. He gets paler every time I see him.

"Don't you ever sleep, Brad?"

"What for?" He seemed genuinely puzzled by my question. I don't think he ever takes a moment's break from his studies, except to go to his night job at the restaurant. He seems convinced he's going to find some new insight into the nature of humanity by uncovering the flaws of the art restoration efforts of the last century. Which means that we're both experiencing the same patterns of creative energy at the moment, though aimed in different directions. Sometimes, we're able to ground each other with a little reality check.

"Just a thought… Have you run this varnish idea past Carter?"

"Not yet. First I've got to get my ducks lined up. It's going to rip holes in that old fossil's theories about the techniques used to create perspective and depth. See, it was all done with the varnish. That's how the musculature was created, not with the watercolors in the frescoes themselves. And the church has been aggressive in ensuring the restoration efforts remove those layers — downplaying the eroticism of the work." His lips were trembling, his eyes bloodshot and enormous.

The last time we'd compared notes on our stress levels, he'd offered me an arsenal of narcotics — to "help you study" — and I'd politely refused. Clearly, he was comfortable using his own product. As for his theory, I'd already heard scholars debate the whole varnish removal controversy ad nauseam. Hadn't Carter himself brought it up in one of his lectures? But before I had a chance to remind Brad of that little oversight, he was tearing into the building. "I've got to get moving on this. See you."

"Hey, wait. Do you know anything about getting the university's lab to test an artifact?"

"Hmm. Don't know. Could take years to set up, I'd imagine, and if it's anything important, they'd never send it to this dump." The books nearly spilled out of his arm as he gestured to the vacant surroundings. "But I know where you can take something on your own. It's gonna cost you, though."

"I don't think I could get permission…"

"Look, I've got to run. But I'll see you tomorrow."

Tomorrow? Oh, crap. I'd forgotten about my shift at the restaurant. "What shift are you on?"

But he was already off. Despite his frantic, crazed energy, he'd been a great support to me in New York. He didn't come from a family of academics like so many of the other students in my program, so he wasn't as pretentious as so many of them. I could hardly fault him for finding a workable way to burn his candle at both ends, however illicit it may have appeared. Plus, he'd gotten me the restaurant gig, which helped pay for life as a student in New York.

Outside, I stood on the corner waiting for the light to change, buried safely in the midtown crowd. Not one of these thousands of people knew how close I was to a major breakthrough.

Heading across 5th, I bumped into Dr. Carter. He looked shaken and confused, struggling to see out of his thick lenses. Recognizing my face as vaguely familiar, he stopped right in the middle of 34th and 5th to have a chat. "Oh, yes, Dave, I was meaning to ask you…"

"Let's cross," I offered, directing him back to the sidewalk I'd just come from.

"I was meaning to ask you if you'd considered looking at Marcus' 1979 study on Romanticism in…" He went on about something that had absolutely nothing to do with my research. I reminded him for the twentieth time this semester that I was Glen and that the subject of my research was the Tarot. "Oh yes, we talked about having you change that."

"I think I may have found that physical evidence you've been asking me to provide, but I may need to do some pigment testing of a rare artifact…"

He didn't attempt to suppress his sigh as he looked at his watch. "I'm so sorry to do this, Glen, but I do have to run. We'll talk about it next week, though I doubt you'll have the time it would take to set up such 'testing'—depending, of course, on the work in question and your personal access to it along with its historical significance. Still, it's unlikely that such a thing would help you in time with the paper you'll be delivering in just under a year's time."

"It's just that this is an amazing opportunity to shed light on an important find…"

"Yes, well, I must run, but we'll talk next week, okay? Have an excellent weekend."

Clearly, I was never going to get enough support from anyone at my university to perform a test on a 15th-century artifact flown in from Italy on the basis of what to them would seem like nothing but a hunch.

Defeated, I went into the only place in New York City where I have come to feel truly safe. A diamond logo bearing the letters E and S split open on a pair of elevator doors, and I slipped between the initials, letting them come together again behind me. Who would ever think to find me in that metal box, hanging from a steel cable in an 86-story shaft? Heading up into the tower of the Empire State Building, I'm as anonymous as it is possible for a human to be.

I always get off on 78. That's where the old man at Steinbacher's Sock Shop holds an eternal sample sale on argyle and plaid. The weathered old man never acknowledges me. In fact, he barely looks at me from his cloudy eyes, as he puts my money into his historic key-punch register with his gnarled hands, asking if I want a bag in a weary tone that suggests he would prefer I say no.

And so I always provide the response he desires, placing my new purchase into my backpack while I look past him to the city stretching before me. For two or three bucks — a small fraction of the price of admission to the Empire State Building's observation deck — I get a semi-private 78th-floor view. We're silent conspirators, the old man and me. To admit that he recognizes me would be to acknowledge he's onto my scheme, visiting him only for the view, and that would invalidate the very existence of his business.

The Empire State Building is the perfect home for has-beens like the old man. The structure gave the city its modern identity, yet it has always been a practical failure itself, built to impress from afar rather than to serve. At first, the building couldn't even get tenants. Now, it swallows the identities of its residents in a mass of steel and plumbing. When I'm inside, I think of the thousands of people working on the floors above and below me: cantankerous magazine editors arguing over a byline, weary immigrant workers toiling in a 39th-floor sweatshop, an elderly janitor pushing a broom down every empty hallway on every floor of the building as he has done each day for the better part of his life... No one pays attention to these secret lives, but I sense them occurring around me, and they diminish my own failures.

Today, as I rummaged through piles of plaids, I tried to focus my efforts. I would have to come up with a definitive thesis within the week or else I'd probably have to end up extending my studies another year — an ugly option, considering my parents' expectations for me to get a job soon.

The old man's blackened eyes squinted suspiciously as I exhaled deeply. I offered an attempt at a smile, which sent his head back immediately into his book. As I stared beyond him over the city, I finally admitted to myself that I have nothing tangible to write about — nothing that will satisfy my thesis requirement, anyway. Looking over the tops of the staggered urban boxes descending like steps from midtown to the base of the Twin Towers at the foot Manhattan, I was once again awed by the invisibility of so many millions of people in this giant abstract tableau.

As confident as I am that I have found a key to the cards' true origins, I told myself, it was going to be nearly impossible to bring these insights to light without a level of support that only a well-respected scholar could reasonably depend upon. Maybe a more realistic option for my thesis would be to take the easy way out and simply reiterate what's already known about the cards' secular origins in a slightly fresh manner — in the same way Steinbacher rereleases his same prints every season with only the barest modifications, all in the name of "keeping up with the latest fashion."

That's not your role. You must listen.

I descended into the subway, resurfacing at the ferry terminal at 8:01 p.m. only to witness the lights of the 8:00 p.m. boat disappearing into the distance. With a half-hour to wait for the next ferry, I sat on one of the hard wooden benches under the long strips of bare fluorescent lights and tried, with little success, to concentrate on my journal, distracted by passengers anxiously pacing the vast, empty room. In this harsh setting, New York was stripped of any glamor, and for a moment I longed to be near my parents in my childhood home, talking with Dad about a favorite movie or book while Mom puttered in the kitchen.

Finally, I departed for Staten Island on a battered orange ferry as it creaked its customary farewell to Manhattan. Each night, I pass the symbol of Lady Liberty. Sometimes I see her as the Queen of Staves, at other times she could be the Hierophant or the Sun. Tonight, she was the embodiment of the Tarot itself, reminding me of my greater purpose.

I would discover and share her story with the world.

Later, 3 a.m.(?)

Back at home, I was just nodding off when the earthen smudge I'd seen in the ancient card's shadows that morning came to mind with a sudden gritty clarity. And just as swiftly, it disappeared, like the memory of a familiar face spotted for a brief moment in a crowd.

Chapter Two

EIGHT OF COINS

A skilled artisan. The creator of elegant objects. Craftsmanship. Great personal effort. A workaholic.

Eight golden circles form two neat rows. Deceptively symmetrical from afar, their carefully crafted opulence shimmers. Wavering irregularities in their buttoned blue borders testify to the humanity of their long-deceased creator.

October 16, 12:30 a.m.

Saturday began as a day of reflection. I woke thinking of my visit to the library the day before as if it had all been some strange dream. Rereading yesterday's journal entry, I wondered if I wasn't reading too much into what I had seen. Maybe I wanted to find an answer so strongly that I was manifesting one.

But the signs are so strong.

It was going to be another busy night at the restaurant, so I needed to spend some time getting myself emotionally and physically prepared to make it a successful one.

I spent the morning in a cleansing meditation in the quiet little park across from my building, listening to the crunch of leaves, feeling the crispness of the approaching winter in the air. Though it was affordable rent that brought me to Staten Island — my apartment was twice as large as anything my classmates renting in Manhattan had found, but a fraction of the price — it was the quiet in the midst of the city that had taught me to love it. I had access to barely frequented green spaces like this one. The color of autumn leaves got me thinking of the ocher pigment in the cards, and I was reminded that whatever presence lies beyond the surface will remain there whether I expose it or not.

It's not time right now.

Perhaps it wasn't time to shed light on the mystery of the cards. Maybe they needed to remain hidden a while longer. When the time was right for revelations, it would present itself.

In the afternoon, I crossed to Manhattan on the ferry, watching the Twin Towers loom before me like a tremendous tuning fork gauging the harmony of the entire city. I would get to Bistro Bordeaux early and start work completely balanced for a change.

Waiting tables is not as easy as I'd thought it would be. Actually, that's a bit of an understatement. Ever since Brad set me up with this part-time waiting gig back in spring, I've been working my ass off just to keep three steps *behind* the full-time servers.

The day I applied, I told the manager that I'd once waited tables at a Greek diner back in high school. I hated to lie, but Brad said it had to be done if I wanted to get in. And working in that cozy little storefront restaurant — bordered by warm wooden trim and tucked away in the teens where Chelsea met the Village — was a coveted gig, pulling in $200 or more per night for the more experienced servers.

So I played it up as best I could. Besides, once I saw the historic photos of New York residents from the twenties and thirties lining the walls, I felt right at home with the energies that had congregated here over the decades. Still, from the knowing look that Carl, our manager, had given me, I'm sure he could figure out just how little experience I had. "You seem very capable," he said. "You'll follow a runner tomorrow." I guess Brad had really sold me.

And that's how I descended into what felt like a lower ring of hell. Only, contrary to Dante, hell was every bit as hot as modern popular mythology would have it. And the only residents more aware of its temperature than those poor lost souls known as servers — condemned as we were to forever drift between the cramped kitchen and the candle-lit dining room — were those confined to the lowest ring, where cooks and chefs stirred cauldrons with giant spoons as they barked out commands in mysterious dialects of Spanish, English, Chinese, and even Arabic.

"Pick 'em up!" shouted the Belgian chef on my first night as plates began piling up in the kitchen. I had all I could do to decipher the scribbles on all the tickets springing up before me with alarming speed. As a vegetarian, I could barely make out the difference between one dish and another. Which one was the rare steak and which the medium filet?

The line cooks just watched me and laughed as if they hoped they'd get to see me drop everything. I fled the burning kitchen into the cool restaurant, my polyester-blend uniform pants already sticking to my sweaty legs, depositing the dishes at what I thought were the correct positions at table 42. "No, I had the veal," said the old man at position B, his weary tone suggesting my little mistake had invalidated his entire dining experience.

Even when customers never complained, I'd sometimes return to the kitchen only to discover that I'd delivered a medium rare burger to the person who'd requested well done. "That was for table 36!" the chef would holler. "Read the fucking tickets!" Each of his explosions was followed by a series of aftershocks, for each of my errors, however small, threw off a whole series of subsequent orders, earning me the wrath of the entire restaurant staff and half of its customers — from the officious waiter who'd placed the order, to the line cooks who had to prepare new corrected meals, to the chef who supervised the whole intricate scene, to the picky old regulars who were convinced they'd been somehow disrespected. Learning to let this negative energy bounce off me, though, has been surprisingly centering.

Over the shifts to come, I came to realize that the anger from the kitchen staff — though not entirely unwarranted — was largely rooted in jealousy over the inequality of our roles. Most of the men who worked there were resentful they'd never been given a chance at the more lucrative role of waiting on tables since English was their second or third or even fourth language. Customers at this place wanted their servers to be fluent in English and proficient in French (or at least sound like it), and I was actually fluent in both thanks to my minor in French literature and a summer in Paris.

And so, despite my lack of serving experience, I fit the image the bistro's customers came for — customers that included film stars and literary giants along with characters from the neighborhood who'd been coming there for decades. I was immediately promoted from runner-in-training to server. At first, I thought the staff's resentment was so deep it would drive me out of the job, until I noticed the touch of respect I was offered in the form of a constant razzing. Their mocking of my mistakes — the same mistakes most any newcomer would have made — were a reluctant admission that I was beginning to take my rightful place within the restaurant hierarchy. I was beginning to find my niche. And the longer I stayed, the more frequent and the more affectionate their jibes became. The challenge was allowing myself to hear the love masked by the confrontational language of our shared environment.

"Pick up these plates now, bonehead!" the chef would shout.

And so went our sweltering ballet between the kitchen and dining room, dancing to the rhythm set by our various masters. It was a dance that was almost entirely physical, removed completely from the academic world of more cerebral considerations. Here, everything was decided in a moment, and thoughtful reflection was the most certain key to failure. If I could master the pace of my role as server, I was sure I could bring just enough of this performance back into my studies to knock my thesis from its inertia.

On this particular night, I didn't mess up any orders or scald myself on the ancient cappuccino machine with its serpentine copper tubing. Nor did I incur the genuine wrath of the chef. In fact, I actually had fun for the first time since I had started working there. At one point, I was actually ahead of my tables and paused in the kitchen to chat with the dishwashers, Issa and Salif, two brothers from Burkina Faso in West Africa.

It seems they'd been working unimaginable hours in two different restaurants for years now, sending money back to their impoverished family. Mooré was their native tongue, they'd told me, but I've taken to speaking to them in French, the lingua franca of their country, though many African languages are still spoken there.

"What do you study at the university, chief?" asked Issa, the taller and more outgoing of the two. He seemed anxious to switch the conversation away from his homeland.

"Art history."

"So you will become a teacher?"

"I'm not sure."

"Americans are so free. They do what they want. They don't decide. They always change."

"I guess that's true." I laughed. "We don't like to be pinned down."

"What art do you research?"

"The Tarot. It's a…" I began to explain but was arrested by the knowing glance the brothers shot each other. They mumbled something in what I presumed was Mooré before I could begin to provide a description.

"Magic," said Issa, as he looked back at me with a smile. The twinkle in his wide, delicate eyes sent a slight chill down my back.

"No, not really magic." I offered to lighten the mood. "They're a kind of game from the Middle Ages, but they can tell you where you're headed."

"Witchcraft," said Salif abruptly, as if dismissing my explanation outright. He'd been so quiet till now that his sudden assertion sent me back a step. Funny, though they called themselves brothers, they hardly resembled one another. Salif's stocky build and coal-black skin made his tall and lanky brother with his much lighter skin look faint and slight. "For you Americans it's a game — a superstition. But it has power."

"So you know the Tarot?" I asked.

They mumbled a few more words in Mooré and *tsked* at each other. "The Tarot is magic," said Salif, increasingly earnest. He put down his dishrag and crossed his squat arms. His eyes were tight, dark, and penetrating. Issa whispered something to him in Mooré.

"I didn't know the Tarot had gained any popularity in Western Africa," I said trying to contain my astonishment. I wasn't prepared to reveal what I'd seen at the library only the day before till I was sure my hunch was correct, and, anyway, I still had to wrap my head around the idea that they seemed to know about the cards.

"Africa is the Tarot's birthplace," Salif added gravely.

"I knew about an ancient Egyptian connection, but I've never heard anything about a connection to the animist religions of the Western part of the continent," I said, alluding to the predominant traditional belief system of hundreds, if not thousands of distinct ethnic groups across the world's most vast continent. Animism, as I understood it, was the belief that there is a living presence in every person, place, and thing — a soul.

There are no coincidences; everything is alive.

"We are Christians."

"But aren't the traditions of animism still practiced in your country?"

The brothers burst out laughing. "Americans are so serious," said Issa. "Even when they play their games, they are very serious." Had they been completely putting me on a few seconds earlier? Were the cards actually present at some point in Africa? Since they had dismissed my last question with laughter, it was awkward to proceed, but I was fascinated to know more. I decided I'd come back to the Tarot with them another time. First, I'd have to gain a bit more trust.

"So how long have you been in the U.S.?" I asked.

"Five years," said Issa.

"Were you the first of your family to come?"

"We have many brothers here," said Issa, smiling. "Now you're our brother too." They took turns shaking my hand, ending the gesture each time by snapping their fingers against mine. It took me a few attempts to master this handshake-snap, which seemed to suggest for them a sort of membership into their brotherhood. As I concentrated on perfecting the exchange, I noticed the small crescent scars along Salif's forearm. Burns? Tribal marks?

I suddenly wondered what the term "brother" constituted for them. Were they literally brothers? In any case, I wasn't sure if calling me "brother" meant that I was somehow considered to be worthy of their friendship or if it was a term used the way Americans tend to say "friend" to refer to everyone from the most intimate soulmate to the most casual of acquaintances. In any case, I had certainly caught their attention, and now I was subjected to their penetrating collective stare.

"Honored to be part of the family." I wasn't sure that really worked the way it came out in French.

"Doesn't anyone speak English around here?" It was Brad. He was taking off his server's apron, having just finished up with his final table.

"Maybe one day you learn Mooré," Issa teased him, exchanging the handshake-snap with Brad.

"Sure, right after I learn Spanish and French and Chinese…"

"Mooré will be language of big business in 21st century," said Salif as he too shared the bonding gesture.

"Yes! And my thesis on varnish in the Sistine Chapel is going to be a national best-seller."

They all laughed.

"Any new insights?" I asked.

"Not since yesterday."

I was really looking for an excuse to talk more about my shot at a breakthrough, but he didn't ask me about my work, and I didn't push further.

"You're getting better out there," he said, commenting on my improved dexterity as a server rather than my life's work. "Gotta run."

"Don't forget to breathe, Brad." But he was out the door before I could offer to teach him a quick exercise I'd learned.

"Americans always in hurry," said Issa. I looked over to share the laughter with him, but he was serious again, his eyes probing once more, as were his brother's.

My brothers.

1:15 a.m.

I caught up on my journal on the foggy ride across the harbor, arriving back home to an urgent message from my father on the answering machine.

"Glen, your mother is in the hospital..." From the tremble in his voice, I knew immediately this was major. "The doctors haven't said what kind of cancer yet, but..."

I was too shocked to process most of the rest. He said that he'd be at the hospital all night with her so I shouldn't call back, but I should start arranging a ticket as soon as possible. I'll have to get him a cellphone...

A flood of images washed over me: the three of us having brunch on the top of the John Hancock building to celebrate Mom's birthday, singing songs on a long road trip down to Florida, launching fireworks and grilling burgers on the patio behind our house...

The distance between Chicago and New York now seems a hundred times greater.

You are going on a long journey.

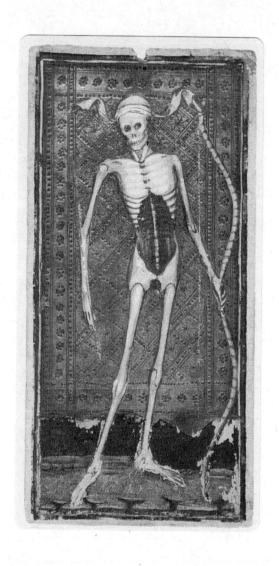

Chapter Three

DEATH

Conflict, obstacles, great struggle and labor, unfinished business, unsatisfied desires. A period of sudden and intense change.

Against the gilded backdrop, his slender white frame is more chalky than ethereal. His hollow eyes and sunken cheeks enhance the irony of his grim smile. A flowing white band tied around his head catches on the top of the twisted staff he holds in his left hand. Perhaps he was once a king or bishop — unless the band is actually a slightly raised blindfold, the snaking staff a giant bow. But there are no arrows, no quiver, just the leering grin and the steady stance. In the distance, the idyllic promise of crisp blue mountains beckons from beneath a golden tapestry of eternity.

October 16, 4 p.m.

Dad said they think it's pancreatic cancer, but they won't know till after surgery. Deep inside the body, the pancreas is at a person's very core, making this one of the most serious operations possible. Of course, the thought of any surgery is disturbing — cutting open a body to remove one of its parts goes against every natural instinct governing the human organism — but a surgery so deep! Just the thought of rubber-gloved hands wielding scalpels and scissors deep inside my mother's open body is an unmentionable violation.

And for all this to come about so suddenly! Dad said she'd been feeling tired these last weeks, and he'd noticed she hadn't had the energy for anything. But it wasn't until the other day that she'd become jaundiced. Then she couldn't get down food. That's when they went to the doctor and the testing began...

And now, here I am on the way to Chicago, feeling as if I'm in a bad dream. Luckily, I have no assignments past due — at least not at this exact moment — and the restaurant was completely accommodating in giving me as much time off as I needed.

Not that any of that matters now. In fact, every time I think of the banality of these daily details in comparison to my mother's fragile life, a hot wave of dizziness passes over me, and my stomach lurches — as in the final moments of a dream in which I'm falling...

Getting closer.

Yes, I had that dream again... Always the same empty hallways going on and on through a vast building. I'm forever running through them, knowing that I'm in great danger, though just around some corner, a door is opening onto a busy street where I'll be safe again. And the whole time, there's this terrible pounding coming from all sides. There's something indescribably threatening about that sound, which penetrates through everything, through the very core of my being. I feel as if I'll explode from the vibrating bass of the terrible noise if I can't find the exit...

Outside the window now, the brutally flat Midwestern landscape approaches. Rows of Monopoly houses — confined within the grid formed by so many wide-lane streets — grow larger by the second. And now our plane is thudding down the runway.

October 19, 9 p.m.

The night I arrived, Dad met me at the gate. From his tousled hair and bloodshot eyes, I could see he hadn't slept in ages. Strangely, though, he looked sturdier than when I'd last seen him months before. "Thank God you're here," he said as he hugged me. "I've had all I could do to keep up with these doctors."

He didn't let go of me as quickly as I'm used to — a steady squeeze replacing the habitual pat on the back. He proceeded to bring me up to date on my mother's condition. Rarely had I seen him so matter-of-fact, so lucid. The severity of the situation had apparently put him into emergency mode, shaving away his humor along with his emotion. There wasn't any time for either just yet. Before he could deal with his own feelings, he had to see to it his wife was being treated properly.

"This operation is a big one," he said on the drive to the hospital. "One of the biggest a person can have."

The ultimate test.

"I read that," I said.

"The chances for success aren't great, and they don't even know for sure what they're dealing with, so we're going to pray for the best, but…"

"Don't get ahead of yourself."

"Are you okay?"

"Yeah, I guess. How about you?"

"I'm better now that you're here." My father had always been the more communicative of my parents. He was the one who could find the words to say what needed saying, and usually without losing his temper.

It was Mom who had trouble expressing her emotions, letting them fester until finally they exploded awkwardly. Suddenly, she'd be screaming that the dishes hadn't been stacked properly in the kitchen or the garbage hadn't been taken out — banalities that indicated she'd felt excluded from the lengthy conversations Dad and I had about books or films. She could never bear the fact that we had so many references in common, while her world was limited to the same daily routine.

Not that Dad hadn't encouraged her to pursue loftier interests than her housework—as a teacher he was far too intelligent to want to confine his wife in a kitchen. But, whether afraid of the challenge presented by the larger world or content with keeping to what she knew, she had restricted her sphere of influence to our household, where her deep love for us sometimes erupted in these little tirades.

Mom expressed herself better outside of language, baking cakes for our birthdays, knitting me a new scarf at the start of each winter, building a bird feeder in the backyard to draw us together as a family around something besides the television. As a child I'd been embarrassed by the almost cliché sentimentality of these gestures, till I finally began recognizing their ritualistic significance.

Sacred symbols.

"I think she's really scared," said my father.

"Who wouldn't be?"

"I know. It's just that I'm not used to seeing her like that."

"True. She's always been so solid."

"Stubborn."

I looked over at him, surprised he'd mention this now.

"Look," he snapped, "just because she's in the hospital doesn't mean she's suddenly a saint."

"Hey, it's okay, Dad."

"Sorry."

"No need to be. You're right."

Mom had always had her ways. Besides, she was a Leo, and her working-class Irish Catholic upbringing on the South Side had instilled habits and rituals in her that she never questioned. You worked hard, you saved up, and you paid your share of dues. That's just how it went, and anything outside of that was a complication best ignored.

The Tarot was simply out of the question. Dad was always curious about my research, but Mom always thought there was something suspicious about "those cards," as she disdainfully referred to them. Hardly a religious fanatic, Mom's faith consisted of going to church on Sunday morning, praying a rosary now and then, and avoiding anything bizarre, especially squares of painted paper that may once have been handled by a medium. Never again did she speak to me about the cards I'd once found among her things, and I dared not bring it up with her for fear she'd think I was accusing her.

"She's so proud of you, you know."

"I guess you're right."

As I got older, I began to realize that all her criticisms over the years had been nothing more than passionate expressions of her love and concern for me, thrown out like weapons in some cases, though always intended to protect and nurture.

But once I'd gone off to grad school, I would return for holidays to find the quiet tension around our dining room table had been replaced with routine questions about my time in New York: "Are you getting enough to eat? Is the neighborhood really safe? I hope you're not taking that ferry at all hours." Increasingly, she seemed to accept that I had grown into adulthood, and that there was little she could do to change that. She seemed quietly resigned to let things proceed as they must.

Let fate take its course.

"She's always loved us so much, you know."

Why did Dad feel the need to explain this now, as if I didn't already know?

"If she ever got mad, it was because she didn't have words to tell us how much."

She had always felt excluded whenever Dad and I would have one of our long discussions. Instead of letting us include her, she'd interrupt every few seconds as if trying to break off the whole conversation. "Want an apple?" she'd ask. Or "It's supposed to be 65 degrees today near the lake." If we stayed on topic, she'd just sigh. "I won't bother you again." She was good at shrinking away, dejected. It was as if she knew she could never truly share the references that bound my father and me so closely.

"It's going to be a shock to see her," my dad warned me.

The next step on your journey.

Tangled in thin white sheets, Mom lay confined between the chrome bars of a hospital bed, awaiting surgery. She looked tiny, jaundiced, emaciated, and completely terrified. It seemed impossible it could have come to this.

"Mom." I held her skeletal body in my arms. God, this was *my* mother. She would be okay. She had to be.

It is almost time.

All those failed efforts to communicate, all those years of broken gestures. They couldn't end like this. That would be impossibly cruel, and things always worked out for the best. Outside the window to her hospital room, a plane left an arching plume of smoke. The journey would be long, but she would make it.

"Is the surgery really necessary?" I'd asked Dad. He said the doctor insisted yes. He'd told Dad there was something like a twenty per cent chance of recovery if it was indeed pancreatic cancer and if it was still at its earliest stage, but I must have heard that number wrong. It must have been a twenty per cent chance of failure. And anyway, it couldn't be cancer, could it?

"You don't have to go through with this, Mom, if you don't want to. We can find alternative treatments."

"I'll give it a try, honey, and we'll see what they can do. If it doesn't work, then let them pull the plug. I'll let them try what they need to, but if I'm just a vegetable with a tube up my nose, stop everything." The tears welled up again in both our eyes.

We said we loved each other about a million times that night and a lot more without uttering another word. Mom had never been one for expressing emotion, so what she did say made it only that much harder. Why would all of this come flooding out of her now unless…

Say goodbye and send her.

But that couldn't be possible. We still had so much to share.

"Remember when I led you and that pack of little brats at St. Mary's on a trip to the science museum?" She seemed to be looking past the water welling up in her eyes and directly back in time.

"I remember, Mom."

Dad and I waited till the morphine kicked in and let her sleep. We went for a long dinner at an Italian place in a strip mall: giant bowls of overcooked pasta with enormous hunks of bread and cheap Chianti. Comfort food, they called it. With tears in our eyes, we laughed over memories of our family vacations.

"Remember when she pulled a tantrum at the Haunted House in Disney over which direction we should tackle the Magic Kingdom to hit the most rides?"

"Yeah," I said. "Then we went our separate ways and she sat there pouting all day by the Tea Cups."

"I think it was Small World."

"Right!"

I suppose an outside observer might have thought we were strange for recalling such tense moments. Maybe it even seemed like we were laughing behind her back. But these bittersweet fragments of memory — when Mom was being cantankerous or controlling — were the ones we remembered the most fondly. Maybe it was because they were the ones when she revealed herself most completely, or maybe it was because a part of us regretted now that we hadn't gone along with her to make everything okay. Would it have killed us to go around the park in the other direction, even if it didn't actually matter which way we went? If Mom hadn't been so insistent and if we hadn't been so inclined to prove her wrong, would these memories have remained so forceful?

Everything is as it must be.

One thing was sure. These memories were the ones only the three of us shared, and if we lost her, it would be only me and Dad who knew of them.

"Our life is going to be changed forever," he said.

"She's going to be fine."

He put his hand on top of mine, but didn't say a word.

We slept little that night. The alarm woke us at 4:00 a.m., and we went right back to the hospital. We sat with her until they came to take her to surgery. She looked even tinier that day than she had the night before, a puffy blue surgical bonnet dwarfing her head. As I hugged her one last time, her eyes teared up again, then the cart rolled away until all I could see was a tiny blue puff disappearing down the corridor.

We waited in that infernal white room for an eternity, listening to the stories of other families. "She's just got to pull through," one of them wailed, though from the look on the faces around him, I suspected that was an unlikely prognosis.

I found it impossible to do much of anything about the texts I'd brought along to study. The characters blurred before me on the page. Flipping through an illustrated book on the Tarot was an even worse idea. The maternal figure of the Queen seemed to appear on every page, her details suddenly invested with a fragility I'd never noticed. Above me, *The Price is Right* on the visitors' television blared false cheer through the waiting room. It seemed unimaginable that I was actually enrolled in a graduate program back in New York City, where I had a job as a server in a restaurant and an apartment in Staten Island.

Home.

The visitors' telephone woke us. It was Mom's surgeon saying the operation was done. We hadn't expected it to be finished for another couple of hours, so this was a bit of a shock. Bad news?

After a barrage of doctor-speak, I understood it hadn't been necessary to remove the pancreas and that chemo was an option now. It wasn't pancreatic cancer after all. The cancer had originated elsewhere, possibly the lymph glands, and had traveled through the body. The pancreas was only one affected area. But since the cancer was wrapped around the pancreas, neither the organ nor the cancer could be removed.

It was only after discussing it with Dad, that I recalled the doctor's other words: "lymphoma" and "rapidly spreading" and "inoperable."

But it couldn't be.

Let it be.

Two hours later, they allowed us into the ICU.

Nothing could have prepared me for the shock of seeing my mother like that. Her head was bloated like some strange wax version of the woman who gave birth to me — a prop mask from a low-budget horror film. A giant tube was stuffed down her throat. I couldn't stay very long in the room with her. In any case, she wasn't conscious.

I went and sat in the waiting room while Dad held her hand. Anxious for something to occupy my mind, I flipped through my reproduction of the old Italian deck. The cards' symbols seemed meaningless, suddenly. I'd always been convinced they could tell a story, but right now even their signifiers seemed empty. They ceased to shimmer.

"Are you okay?" my father asked me when he emerged.

"Sort of. It's just that when I walked in there, the first thing I thought of was what she said this morning. She didn't want to end up like a vegetable with a tube down her throat and…"

"She needs to rest."

"I know, but the cancer is…"

"We're going to lose her."

I only remember the echo of the hallway, then the tiled floor coming closer, then my father's arms around me. The lights of passing cars flashed past me outside the window. And soon we were home, sitting on the balcony of my parents' high-rise condo, overlooking the relentless landscape of suburban strip malls and trimmed square lawns.

I traced out the steps before us to better cope with them. "Once she recovers from the operation, they'll want her to take chemo, and she'll have to decide about that. I can make a few calls and find out about holistic methods…"

"We'll have just enough time to make our peace with her and say a proper goodbye. But it's going to be a tough road ahead. Anyway, there's nothing we can do about it tonight. Are you okay?"

He poured us both scotch and we drank till we could shut down enough to sleep for a few hours.

Another step on your journey.

The next day Mom still looked awful, but it was a hell of an improvement over the night before. She was able to look at me and mumble my name. There were so many things we all wanted to say, but only "I love you" seemed right. And yet those three words, the most powerful ones in the language, seemed useless now.

We spent a lot of that and the next day traveling between the waiting room and the cafeteria. Once we went to a Greek diner about four blocks away where a glass case full of over-glazed deserts forever turning in the refrigerated interior stood like a sentry at the door. The food was even nastier than the floral wallpaper and gilded mirror hangings suggested it might be. "If I had to guess why there's a higher incidence of certain cancers in this part of the country," I said, "I'd point to the food in these diners before blaming waste dumping at industrial laboratories."

"Don't be so sure the two industries haven't worked out a mutually beneficial deal."

"Good point." We allowed ourselves a chuckle, which felt about as comforting as a chocolate stolen from a child.

"You should go back to New York."

"But, Dad!"

"The doctor made it clear to us this morning that she's going to be resting for a while before she has the strength for the chemo, then she's going to be out of it again for a while. I'm going to need you here at the end..."

"Dad, she's going to be fi — "

"She's dying, Glen. Listen to me. I want you to go back to school and get ready to come back when I need you."

Find your place.

I am swooping down again over the billion twinkling lights of New York City. In a few hours, I'll be adding one more light to that illuminated tapestry when I switch on my desk lamp in Staten Island and get down to work. If my mother is dying, then I must make her death mean something as her only child. I will leave a legacy to preserve her memory and make her proud.

Go.

Chapter Four

THE HERMIT

Possessor of secrets. The withholding of knowledge. Circumspection. Self-denial, withdrawal. Regression, caution.

Though not yet defeated, he is approaching the end of his journey. Leaning forward with the support of a long cane, his entire robust mass seems focused on something far in the distance. From beneath a golden, multi-tiered hat, his searching eyes are black and piercing — in stark contrast with his flowing white beard, which mirrors the color of the sands in the hourglass he holds out before him like a lantern. He is draped in a tremendous deep-blue robe. Clearly, he is a man of carefully calculated measurements. Some might call him Father Time, emerging from the depth of the dark void with only the cautious wisdom of a single, narrow perspective to guide him.

October 20, 10:30 p.m.

The long commute from LaGuardia Airport last night — from bus to subway to ferry — eased me back into my New York life. I couldn't stop thinking of Mom in the hospital, but already the weight of my unfinished thesis was bearing down on me again.

Let it happen.

By the time I was back in my apartment, Chicago had slipped almost completely away, and this morning, the whole trip seemed like nothing but a strange dream. Could my mother really be dying? I didn't like to think of that. For now, I didn't have to. I would just follow Dad's advice and get everything in order.

I went straight to the university to see Dr. Carter.

"I'm on to something big," I blurted out when he opened his office door. I hadn't intended to speak so directly about my discovery, but it just came out of me in his presence.

No secrets. No accidents.

"There's a card here in New York from Bergamo. It's not supposed to leave Italy, but a private collector wants it tested. I've actually seen it, and its pigment can't possibly be from the 15th century."

"Slow down." He invited me into his cramped office and offered me a seat before squeezing in behind his old wooden desk, piled with the requisite papers. On all sides, the walls teetered with old books — as obligatory for a man of his tenure as the framed degrees hung between them. My eyes landed on the spine of a book on da Vinci, and I took that as I sign that my intuition was grounded in possibility. "What card?" asked Dr. Carter.

I hadn't meant to go down that path. Not without more of a coherent story to tell.

"It's the Page of Staves from the Visconti-Sforza deck. There's a paint chip revealing a sort of earthen pigment I suspect is from… Well, it can't be from Europe, not at that time."

His fingers formed a tent in front of his mouth as he contemplated me silently. The pause grew heavy. He was waiting for me to say more, but I didn't have anything else to give him. For the first time, he seemed to be listening to me, regarding me as a person worthy of consideration. "Well, what have you got?" his engaged silence seemed to say. But I didn't have enough to repay the attention he'd invested in me.

Until now, I'd blamed him for dismissing me because of the cards, but I realized that I'd been just as guilty of dismissing him. Though he was no longer at the peak of his career, he'd once been at the top of his field and was still a widely consulted authority on matters of art history. I hadn't given him the respect he had earned or taken advantage of his knowledge.

Listen to the voices when they speak to you.

"It sounds to me, my dear boy, like you haven't a clue which direction your thesis will take."

I found myself numb, incapable of replying. I'd really blown it.

"One interesting artifact does not a thesis make," he continued. "You must consider the broader relevance…"

"Dr. Carter, I know I saw something that will prove the cards are connected to traditions far older than the Renaissance. But I need you to request a pigment test be conducted on the card from Bergamo."

"That's quite a tall order for such a vague proposition based on what sounds like nothing more than a hunch."

"It's more than a hunch," I said firmly, staring him straight in the eye. "I know it can be measured with carbon dating or inconsistencies in brush strokes or painting techniques or pigments… I'm not sure exactly what yet, that's true, but I will find the quantifiable source to back up my intuition." I was shaking.

Dr. Carter had pulled back. His eyes scanned me like one of the artifacts he'd spent his career studying. "Glen, I think you're going to have to file for an extension…"

"Actually, that's what I came to you to talk about." I hadn't even mentioned my mother, which was the main reason I'd come to him in the first place. Once I had explained the situation to him, everything else receded into the background.

"Glen, I'm so sorry. By all means, you must take however much time you need…"

"But the card…"

"Don't worry about that."

"It will only be at the Pierpont Morgan library until the collector has finished."

"Why don't I look into it for you while you're away? Yes, I'll give a call over to my colleague Barry Levi at the library."

"That would be great. I know you won't be disappointed."

Was he actually intending to act on my "hunch," as he called it, or was he just getting me out of there, afraid the stress of my mother's illness was too much for me?

Let it happen the way it must.

On my way downtown to the restaurant, the subway stalled one stop early at 14th Street. I'd been meant to get out there, I decided.

Wandering through the streets of Greenwich Village, I lost myself in the neighborhood's antique shops, and for a few hours, neither my thesis nor my mother's illness existed, as I browsed through quirky old collections of objects charged with stories.

And there, on the top of a stack of books haphazardly piled in the corner of a dusty bookstore, I found the text that could very well be the key to unlocking the future direction of my work: *Les origines africaines du tarot.* When I saw the title, I knew that everything up to now had prepared me for this moment, and that my instincts had guided me well.

You are ready to receive.

There was no question I was meant to have it, so I didn't even open it in the store except to read the price on the first blank page. At $17 I could hardly complain about the yellowing pages and battered cover. I slipped it straight into my backpack after paying and saved the pleasure of discovering its contents for later.

It was early afternoon by the time I got to Bistro Bordeaux, about an hour before the other servers would arrive to set up for dinner. Peering in, I saw no signs of life, so I rapped on the ivy-framed window. Salif's round face instantly filled the space on the other side of the glass, and I jumped back, startled. He gave me an intense, disapproving stare, making no move to open the door. Then his eyes widened with recognition. "Ah, chef! C'est Monsieur Glen."

He opened the door and extended his hand, taking me through the West African handshake he and his brother had taught me. "How are you, Glen? And how is your family? And how are your studies?" He rattled off a long series of questions about my health and well-being in what he had explained to me was the traditional African style.

I responded in the same African tradition, saying all was well when it really wasn't, asking instead how he and his family were doing. Salif and Issa had told me that pretty much anywhere on the continent of Africa, it was best not to complain. Even if you were literally on death's door, you always said, "I have my health." To do otherwise was to be a burden on the community and a sign of weakness.

I thought suddenly of the book buried in my backpack and wondered if its pages might contain anything that wouldn't make sense to me, having never been to Africa. It was surely no accident that the paths of our lives had crossed. These co-workers of mine might become interpreters leading me to other important answers.

Listen to the voices.

"Glen! Welcome back." I'd been about to ask Salif if he'd ever heard of the Tarot when Carl, our manager, emerged from the kitchen. "How did everything turn out? Is your mom going to be okay?"

"It's cancer. We're not sure what the next step will be, but we're pulling through." It occurred to me that even though we answered such questions more directly outside of Africa, we still skirted the deeper emotions involved, so we weren't really so different after all.

"Oh, my god, I'm so sorry, Glen. Shouldn't you be with her?"

"I will be. I just came back to take care of a few things. And I came to ask you…"

"Of course! Take all the time you need."

I'd intended to work a few more shifts, but he insisted I take the time off. So, now I am free to return whenever I need to.

As I left, Salif caught my eye. "*Wend na kod laafi,*" he said in Mooré. "May you have health." He took my hand in his and slipped a piece of paper in it. "A picture," he said. "From Burkina Faso."

"Where did you get it?"

"You have so many questions."

He smiled and turned back to the kitchen.

It wasn't until I was sitting on the ferry that I took a good look at the gift Salif had given me. The earthen tones of the hand-painted image, which was about the size of a modern playing card, had faded into each other, so it was hard to make out. In broad, crude brush strokes, it depicted a man with pinkish cheeks holding a little black box… a camera. It was a little painting of a white tourist visiting Africa.

I hear the creaking of the fender piles now as our boat docks on Staten Island. I was so lost in catching up on this journal that I didn't even feel the boat lurching back and forth as it approached the dock.

A long journey lies ahead.

2 a.m.

My head is spinning. What I've read so far in *The African Origins of the Tarot* has blown me away. There are so many clues for unraveling the secret to the mystery of the cards' images and structure that I can scarcely believe I haven't dreamed this book into existence.

Of course Dr. Carter would say I've got nothing but my own intuition to indicate the book isn't merely the rantings of a charlatan. One huge problem with the manuscript is that its publisher, Griot Press, seems to be virtually untraceable. Not only does the book fail to list an address for the publisher, but an Internet search for the name turns up nothing either. There isn't even a date of publication given, though if this were a first edition, I'd guess it was published in the eighties based on the condition of the manuscript. The word "griot" itself refers to a West African storyteller, a role that seems to function a lot like that of a court jester in medieval Europe.

The Fool.

From its awkward usage of fonts and dozens of typing mistakes, not to mention its sloppy binding and thin paper stock, the text would, at first glance, seem to have been published independently, possibly at the expense of its author, Abdou Ouédrago. A search for him turns up nothing either, though the name Ouédrago seemed to be fairly common in Burkina Faso, where Salif and Issa are from.

Never any accidents.

If the book had been published in West Africa, that would explain its failure to conform to Western publishing conventions. As for the book's contents, it provides a completely original argument for the Tarot originating in West Africa, attributing the cards' invention to African shamans who used them as visual tools in healing ceremonies. The first cards, says the author, were strips of bark painted with natural pigments.

Ouédrago says the cards date back to the "dawn of African civilization," which he claims to be "dream worlds away from European culture." He never traces a definitive path from the shamans' cards to the more modern European decks, though he claims "The cards moved into the home of the white man when he left Africa to take her people into slavery."

The historical passages are far from fleshed out in the kind of language and references that would be acceptable to most Western academics, and the appearance of Tarot-like cards in a remote West African community with limited exposure to modern European society is hardly evidence of their presence in that same community in ancient times. But what is astonishing are the photographs of what he calls the "true" Tarot, taken by Ouédrago himself in the late sixties in a secluded part of the continent near the reclusive Lobi people.

These photos — many overexposed or out of focus — give at least a sense of the pressed bark "cards," some of them adorned with shells and feathers and all painted with crude images that vaguely resemble figures from the Major Arcana: a four-wheeled cart (the Chariot?), an elderly figure with some sort of staff or cane (the Hermit?), a bright crescent (the Moon?).

The figures are drawn with broad, almost caricaturized strokes. Some might say they are examples of "primitive" art, but there's something far more precise about them. Primitive work tends to represent the universal, relying on ambiguity to allow for many possibilities, while each of these images has what I can best describe as a definite personality.

Ouédrago says that there were twenty-two such painted pieces of bark in all, though photos of only ten of the cards — or *Naarem*, as he calls them — are featured in the book. It would be hard to imagine manipulating twisted pieces of bark in the same way one shuffles and cuts modern cards. Indeed, Ouédrago argues that the concept of the "deck" was introduced by Europeans in a corruption of the original African concept of the *Naarem*, which treated each strip of bark as a separate entity. But while in animist culture every object is believed to be alive, the *Naarem* were supposedly animated with several additional levels of consciousness. The natural pigments used to paint the cards included the *blood of sacrificial animals*, contributing, supposedly, to the divinatory powers of the cards by providing a link to the spirit world of the dead.

I hadn't dared admit it to myself, let alone write it down until now, but what stunned me when I first saw the original gilded Italian cards in the library, was the resemblance of that elusive smudge across the Page of Stave's pale cheek to dried blood.

The life force running through it.

By the time I'd read this far into Ouédrago's text, I realized it was dark outside. I had charged straight home from the ferry and never once took my nose out of the book. When I finally looked around the room, I saw the answering machine blinking. It was Dad. He said Mom was stable. Strange, but I don't feel concerned about her at the moment. I feel like she's resting and doesn't need me.

You'll know when it's time.

Plus, I couldn't take my mind off the African text. Where had it come from? Maybe the store I'd purchased it from could tell me more. I found the receipt in the bottom of my backpack but it contained no more than the numeric digits of the transaction that had put the book into my possession. Perhaps the numbers themselves were significant. But first I had other leads.

I went online and searched for bookstores in Greenwich Village. My initial search led me to a page on historic districts in New York, and I found myself exploring a different direction than I had intended to, coming to a site that listed historic homes in New York preserved as museums. A few clicks later, I stumbled upon a photo of a parlor that looked like something out of a 19th-century séance.

Follow where you are taken.

Apparently the home was located in the East Village and housed a minor museum called the Trader's House. That would be easy to visit on my next trip to Manhattan. On the museum's site were photos of the plush front parlor in the former residence — its windows draped with velvet tasseled curtains, its walls hung with gas sconces.

The site had a page of links to related articles and so on. I browsed for a while. There were stories about period costumes and furnishings, along with the inevitable ghost story. Sadly, museum curators seem intent on making a joke of the supernatural, creating "spooky" events for Halloween rather than opening themselves and their visitors up to the energies in their midst.

But there was a lot of excellent content on their site too, including a feature about 19th-century parlor life in New York. And there, in a list of popular parlor games of the period, along with chess, Old Maid, Dr. Busby, and charades, was "The Ancient Egyptian Game of

Nared." The spelling was slightly different from the word cited in the Ouédrago text, but surely it wasn't a coincidence.

Not that the reference to Egypt was unusual. After the Tarot had become popularized in France during late 18th century, occultists like Gébelin had spread the idea the cards were rooted in some ancient, mystical tradition from the earliest Egyptian civilization. It was a theory most art historians argued had come entirely from popular fashion.

At a time when European colonizers stole ancient artifacts from Egypt and shipped them back to Europe, Europe's romance with ancient Egypt reached a fever pitch. Egyptian revival fantasies crept into Western architecture, literature, fashion, and, inevitably, spiritualism. Soon the influence hopped the pond. The pyramid was "in."

So it was no surprise to see Egyptian themes in card games of the period, but for that strange word I'd only come upon for the first time that morning to appear again…

Naarem.

I thought back to my first encounter with ancient Egypt, exploring the dusty basement collection at The Field Museum while growing up in Chicago. Long before I'd ever discovered the Tarot, I'd been mesmerized by those ancient mummies in their gilded boxes — their alabaster Canopic jars lined neatly behind the smudged glass of old display cases. It was easy, in retrospect, to justify my fascination with their colorful, cartoon-like forms and painted facades. What kid didn't love something that sparkled so brightly and offered just the right touch of morbid fantasy? To think they'd pulled the brains out through the nose!

It occurs to me now that my love of ancient Egypt was probably deeper than that experienced by most children. My eye had been drawn by something greater than the golden shimmer of King Tut's mask. My curiosity had gone way beyond a common fascination, and I would reread entire books on the ancients from cover to cover, dreaming myself back in time. What exactly had so drawn my attention then? Is that what had led me to the Tarot now?

Whatever it was, it was the same thing — no, the same *force* — that was stirring me now, drawing me to that museum in the East Village. There had to be a reason why I was led to find it.

Listen and follow.

Chapter Five

THE MOON

Dishonesty, deception, trickery. Bad influence, ulterior motives. Insincerity, craftiness, slander. Falling into a trap.

She stands on the edge of the steep cliff. Her feet are bare. In her left hand is a broken bow, bent and tangled into two serpent-like wisps; in her right, a moon. She brings the moon towards her face at an impossible angle, as if she has stretched past the limits of her human form to pluck it from among the stars. Staring into the crescent's bluish-white light, she lets it cast deep shadows under her puffed eyes, which are pinched in the corners. Perhaps she is struggling to prevent her tears from overflowing, or perhaps she is hatching a vengeful plot. The pattern on the hemline of her disheveled dress lines up perfectly with the top of the shadowy mountain range in the distance. She may have lost something important in the material world, but she is at one with nature and will use its mysteries to obtain whatever she wants.

This morning, I woke to that dream again… Racing down endless corridors, being pursued by someone I couldn't see. There's a sense of urgency to the dream that goes beyond a desire to save myself from death. It's as if I'm racing against a clock that has already been set to make me late. Whoever is chasing me will catch me, I know, and that's when I feel the floor go out from under me, and I jolt awake.

Once I was up, I couldn't bring myself to focus on my work, so I took an impromptu trip to the museum in the East Village I'd discovered on the Internet.

Extraordinary that such a building had managed to survive intact, while the world shot up around it. Sandwiched today between a garage and a vacant lot, the relatively modest structure has retained its original exterior for nearly two centuries, even as crowded tenement buildings around it were converted into luxury co-ops and more opulent neighboring residences were either looted or tumbled or both. Falling somewhere in between these extremes, this particular home, a merchant's "uptown" family dwelling (for it had been built at a time when only the tip of Manhattan was densely populated), had passed through centuries unscathed.

Entering between the ivory columns adorning the front door, I met my guide, Eileen. Not only was she beautiful, but she was so engaged in describing the story of the home's contents that I found myself mesmerized. Her dark eyes sparkled when she spoke about the former inhabitants of this meticulously preserved space.

I wondered if this was how I came across to others when I spoke of my interest in the Tarot. If so, I could imagine how people could find it unsettling, though for me, Eileen's enthusiasm was invigorating — affirming, in fact. Beyond her stunning beauty, there was something almost ethereal about her — luminous. At first glance, she was downright haunting, but then a fragility emerged from somewhere beyond the dark eyes. Maybe it was the size of her tiny white hands that suggested delicacy, or maybe it was the slight creases at the corners of her red mouth that made her seem slightly vulnerable.

"With only a few exceptions, all of the furnishings and fixtures you'll see throughout the home are original to the building," she informed me proudly, buttoned up in her coal-black docent attire in the strictest 19th-century style, "brought here by the family that had owned it for generations."

"Stunning," I said. "Too bad you don't have more visitors."

"People tend not to notice it here when they're rushing off somewhere. It's kind of hidden." She was blushing a bit as she made what sounded like excuses, and I got the sense that she preferred the museum home to remain her own little secret. I could imagine her sitting alone in the front parlor laced in period costume, working on a bit of needlepoint or peering at a faded image of the people who once lived there through the antique stereoscope near the fireplace. The further the house remained sheltered from all modernity, the better she would be able to cushion herself in her fantasy of the time it represented.

Not that I minded. In fact, I preferred to have it all to myself with her on this lazy day of pushing all other tasks aside. I breathed in the rich smell of the old wooden walls and tried to imagine the previous inhabitants laughing as they ran up and down the steep creaking stairs, igniting the gas fixtures suspended from the ceilings with long brass lighters, slipping a coal-filled bed warmer beneath the lumpy blankets to chase the chill away before sleep.

The home's most recent inhabitants, two daughters of the wealthy merchant who had built it, were reclusive spinsters who'd remained holed up there long after their father had died. In fact, the two of them grew old and died in the place, never much changing its décor, even as the world outside evolved at a frantic pace. It was thanks to their reluctance to engage with the big city emerging around them that these two sisters had kept the pincushion settee in the front parlor for "entertaining" guests and the closets upstairs stuffed with tiny Victorian dolls with pinched porcelain faces. These were not museum pieces, only bits of the sisters' lives.

"What sorts of games did they play?" I asked, hoping to hear about the Tarot.

"The sisters didn't leave much evidence of their interest in parlor games of the period, though there is some mention in their diaries of charades. They were more taken with sewing and baking."

"Was there no mention of playing cards or the Tarot?"

"Not that I know of, but you might return another time and speak with Grace, who actually does most of the research on the collection here at the museum."

"On the web site, there's something about the Ancient Egyptian Nared."

Was it just me, or had she stiffened when I made reference to the game? "Oh, yes, I remember reading something about that, but as far as I know, we don't actually have the game itself. I believe it's another reference to a diary entry from one of the sisters, but again, Grace would be the one to ask."

"When would she be in?"

"She's here at least twice a week and always at volunteer trainings."

"Are you looking for volunteers?" Maybe that way I could get an insider's view of the game. Perhaps there were even artifacts locked away in the attic that weren't available to the general public.

"Are you a big history buff?"

"I'm actually working towards a degree in art history. "

"You'll definitely want to meet her, then. I'm sure she'd love to have you apply for a volunteer docent position." She hadn't stopped blushing, and I realized now that she was smiling. Was she inviting me to join her in understanding the mysteries of this house? "In fact, the next training is on Sunday at noon."

"I'm not sure I could take that on right now."

"You could always attend the training and decide afterwards if you want to work a shift or not. I'm sure you'd find it fascinating."

As she spoke, I looked over her shoulder to study a picture of the sisters, their whalebone corsets securely fastened, draining away the oxygen away from their pallid cheeks, their sharp black eyes confronting the camera as if daring it to find an impropriety. I was astonished at how close to us they seemed, their presence reaching out through the images and objects they had left behind.

They are still here.

"It's not often we get someone so interested in the house," she said, as she accompanied me to the exit.

"I feel a connection to things from another time, even if it's not quite the time I'm studying."

"I'm always finding that connection…especially in this house."

"Would you like to get together for coffee…"

"Sure!" She pushed a strand of her fine black hair away from her eyes and behind her ear. As she smiled, she exhaled slightly, as if she'd been holding her breath. I found myself doing the same. It looked like we had a date.

"Here's my number," I said.

"Are you free tomorrow?" she asked.

"Just studying, but I can always break away for a minute."

"Let's meet at Café Angelico at 5:00."

"Where's that?"

"At 54 East 3rd Street, between 1st and 2nd."

"Hells Angels block?"

"I can see you know your city."

"I'm looking forward to it."

"Me too."

I sat outside on the top deck of the ferry on my way home and delved back into *The African Origins of the Tarot*, coming across a fascinating passage about the use of Naarem in healing ceremonies. The marabout (or "priest"), it seems, lays out three of the cards in a triangular fashion around the hearth of the sick person, with the point of the triangle aimed toward the door. As the hearth is the center of the African household, it is the place where all grounding and healing begins. By facing the cards toward the entranceway, the marabout is inviting the bad spirits to leave. The two sides of the triangle that point towards the entrance represent the methods (spiritual and physical) by which the spirits must be removed, while the base of the triangle represents the evil that has infected the sick individual.

Ouédrago witnessed one such cleansing rite, which terminated in the beating of a "witch" — the allegedly unfaithful wife of a man who had suddenly and mysteriously fallen sick — to her death. The author offered no additional details and made no effort to investigate further, merely accepting the deadly judgment of the marabout as fair and just. "The stricken man was immediately cured following the witch's extermination," Ouédrago concluded routinely, never addressing the cruel treatment of the woman. I was left wondering about the author's ability to objectively interpret and analyze his subjects.

Just let it be.

From there, the book drifted into very general chapters about basic beliefs of animists across Western Africa and the world. According to the central teachings of animism, it seemed, each object in nature had its own spirit that needed to be respected and treated properly to preserve the natural balance of the universe.

There were only a few references to the actual cards themselves throughout the remainder of the volume, and those were little more than repetitions of material covered in the first and second chapters.

I found my thoughts wandering as I tried to focus on the text. Soon, I was watching the buildings of Manhattan recede into the distance. I imagined each of them infused with a soul. Or were they formed of many souls? Perhaps each of the parts that made up these buildings — steel and glass and concrete — was infused with its own private divinity. Did the spirits within the natural materials used to form these "man-made" structures continue to thrive and pulsate within their towering new forms? Or had they been chopped into pieces and reassembled into a form that prevented them from taking on their optimal properties? Could it be that man had insulted nature by turning its divinities into these rigid structures, and could modern atrocities such as war and genocide be best explained as a spiritual retaliation to man's manipulations?

No matter what sort of perversion of nature had been required to build New York, it remained for me one of the most fascinating spectacles on the planet. And I wondered how long before it, like all great cities, collapsed.

Everything is natural.

After the ferry bumped into the dock on Staten Island, I walked through the parting steel gates with the thousands of strangers around me and walked up the steep sidewalk towards the deli nearest home. Manhattan was now little more than a tiny strip of glitter in the distance. I bought a carton of juice and a loaf of bread, then continued up the steep hill, past the drugstore and pizzeria, to my apartment. From my window, Manhattan seemed all but swallowed up by the great harbor. Yet it shimmered so brightly as the sun set, as if powered by the billions of radiant souls who had inhabited it over the centuries.

While dinner heated in the microwave, I called Dad. I had put him and Mom out of my mind to try and settle my emotions, but I couldn't put them off any more.

"She's in a lot of pain, but the doctors say she's healing well. For the time being, she's mostly just sleeping, so there's no reason for you to be here."

"What about you?"

"I'm fine. I'll need you later, but right now I'm fine." We decided I'd return to Chicago in a week. By then Mom would be home, and strong enough, hopefully, to appreciate visitors. I tried insisting I come sooner, but he said it was best this way. "It will probably be the last time you'll see her," he said. "So you should be here when she's awake enough to really visit with you…"

"Dad, let's not get ahead of ourselves. Just wait and see how it goes."

"It's only a question of time, Glen, and you're going to need to be ready."

I didn't want to get into it with him over the phone, so I just promised to book something online that evening and hung up, feeling completely drained by his negativity. I know that he's only trying to protect me and himself by preparing for the worst, but maybe he's actually changing her fate by not believing the most complete recovery is possible.

You must believe.

I booked a ticket to Chicago for exactly one week from today to have something on the schedule. Just having the date on the calendar makes me feel closer.

Then I pulled out the cards. Not surprisingly, they said a journey was coming up in the near future. They also spoke about lessons from the past. Mom seemed to appear in the form of the Moon, which is normally a card of deception or trickery. I think she has fallen prey to believing what the doctors are telling her and giving up on life. I have to get to her before she loses hope. It was meant for me to be away from her so I could learn to understand there's still hope.

Just believe.

Chapter Six

FIVE OF CUPS

The aftermath of a fit of madness. Partial loss, regret. Superficial friendship, delayed inheritance, new alliances. Imperfection.

Four golden goblets form two parallel rows. A fifth lies on its side, breaking the image's symmetry. Perhaps the artist was overly generous in rounding these bulbous vessels, leaving no space in which to keep the fifth standing on its thick octagonal base. Or perhaps the fifth goblet has been deliberately inverted. No liquid spills from its bright mouth, so there is no sense of loss. There is, however, a sense of emptiness, enhanced by the thick tangle of vines snaking between the containers, barricading them from each other.

A strange day of falsely heightened expectations. It started when I woke in the middle of that same deeply unsettling dream.

Even if I'm not consciously thinking about it, the dream always stays with me somewhere deep inside. There's that incessant pounding of the footsteps, forever pursuing me through the interminable hallways. I pass dozens of doors, all of them locked tightly, though I never have to try any of the knobs to know for sure. And scattered in the dust on the floor are rectangular bits of paper, which could very well be Tarot cards, only they are all face down, so I can never be sure.

But I must keep moving — of that I have no doubt or hesitation — until I come upon the old wooden staircase resembling the one in the Trader's House. Had my visit yesterday embellished the dream, or have I always dreamed of it in such detail? I can no longer remember the way I saw it before, only the immediacy with which it haunts me now.

Let it guide you.

Once I shook the mood of the dream, my thoughts drifted to Eileen. To think that I'd been drawn to the museum while searching for the Tarot and had simply happened upon it, and then to have visited the museum on a whim, arriving precisely while she was the only one on duty with no other visitors were around…

Destined to meet.

I didn't want to get my hopes too high, though, and made myself keep busy. I spent most of the day trying to draft an actual outline for my thesis. If I had *something* down on paper it would hopefully free my mind a bit when I went back to Chicago in a week.

I figured I'd start by taking inventory of what I had learned so far, beginning with a quick overview of all the existing histories of the Tarot I'd been able to locate. The only ones accepted (or even partially accepted) by academics were those written by Kaplan, Guiles, Decker, Depaulis, and Dummett.

Much energy had been devoted in these writings to debate over the origins and intentions of the cards, though the techniques employed in the creation of the actual *objects* were all but ignored, even in the most respected texts on the subject. The cards had been cataloged, situated on timelines, and positioned on geographical maps, but clearly not enough attention had been given to their texture, shading, and composition. Was form not a critical component of the cards' function? How then could the one be studied without the other?

As for what had been written about the actual physical makeup of the cards, I could turn up only a few theories and even fewer hard facts.

The most popular topic of investigation was the possible symbolism hidden in heraldic devices that had been incorporated into the cards. Had the 14th- and 15th-century Milanese nobles who'd commissioned the decks requested that their family crests be integrated into the imagery because they believed there was something sacred about the cards and that being depicted in them offered some sort of divine power? Had they believed they were writing themselves into some ancient map of the unconscious? Or were they merely entertained by the idea of appearing in their own personalized parlor game?

Other Tarot theorists wrote about what the introduction of back designs and watermarks in later centuries might have represented. Was there hidden symbolism in the infinitely repeating diamonds and lozenges on the backs of French cards from the 18th century? Were the subliminal watermarks communicating more than just the name of the manufacturer? Were the government tax stamps that once sealed boxes of 19th-century playing cards a quiet, official acknowledgement of the cards' powers? And what of Tarock, Minchiate, Tarocco Siciliano, and even modern playing cards? Were these Tarot spin-offs? Or was one of them the "real thing"?

On and on went the stream of theories and questions, but the only thing that approached an actual investigation of techniques employed in the painting of the earliest cards was the occasional casual reference to their style being influenced by Renaissance masters like Bembo and Giotto, though there was no evidence such masters participated directly in the cards' creation.

I hadn't been able to find any published research on the actual pigments used in the cards, nor was there anything in the available literature about the artists who'd been commissioned to create them, let alone the instruments or techniques they used in the process.

In short, I was acknowledging for the first time on paper just how precarious a position I was in. First of all, I was still a long way off from completing enough research on my subject to come up with a coherent thesis. Basically, my only solid and original idea was contingent upon finding something revelatory in sampling the pigment from a single card, and for this I was depending entirely on Dr. Carter's ability to secure access to it. What if he wasn't able to get the necessary permissions? Or worse, what if pigment testing actually disproved my theory?

The answer is right in front of you.

The truth is that I didn't really know what I wanted to say. While I sensed that the mystical connection to the cards that academics had been so quick to discount was a real one, I needed some tangible proof of what was essentially intangible. Was academia the best place to make such arguments? Was I wasting my time? And how was I supposed to care about working out all these details with my worries about Mom always in the background? Maybe I would have to take a leave of absence. But that would mean another year of school in New York.

Discouraged, I tried focusing on my date with Eileen — yes, it was only coffee, but I decided to believe in myself enough to think positively and assume the best. Even from our first meeting, I felt a real connection with her, and I hadn't been able to stop thinking of her brooding eyes, her bashful smile.

As I exited the subway in the East Village, I had only a couple of minutes to put all the stress and worry behind me. I wandered past the museum on my way to the café. It was hard to imagine the plush, formal interior of that historic structure while standing outside it on a filthy New York sidewalk teeming with leaking black garbage bags. I found myself wishing I could go inside and close off the modern world, following the steps up to the attic where everything would be so quiet, so protected.

At home.

Lost in these thoughts, I crossed the Bowery, where out of the corner of my eye I saw someone familiar: a tall slender figure shaking with laughter. It was Issa, the more jovial of the two Burkinabe brothers who worked with me at the restaurant. He was in front of a particularly dilapidated old funeral parlor talking to…was it Brad? He had the same build and the same anxious way of carrying himself, never able to stand still for a second, his arms gesticulating as he spoke, but his face was turned in such a way that it was always blocked by Issa or another random person passing by. I was about to wave, but they disappeared into the building, though not before Issa had a chance to slip something to the other man in what looked like a velvet pouch.

I crossed the street to get a better look into the funeral parlor, but there was no way to look inside without going through the front door, and that would have made it seem like I was spying on them. How weird that they should be meeting there of all places. What could they be exchanging? None of my business, I guess, but strange nonetheless.

The answers will come.

The café where I was to meet Eileen was supposedly only a few blocks further. I found the street, but approaching number 54, I saw nothing but a former tenement building sandwiched between the others. Cherubic angels with hollow eyes adorned the space under its gated windows.

It was just down the block from the Hells Angels clubhouse, between 1st and 2nd, but there was no café at that address. A few doors down, there was a nondescript place called the Internet Café. I went in. No Eileen. A heavily tattooed server with a tangled red goatee said he had never heard of a Café Angelico. I called information from the payphone on the corner. None listed in Manhattan — or in any of the five boroughs for that matter. Nice.

I went back to 54 and scanned the buzzers. The name at number three was "Angel." Short for "Angelico," maybe? Had Eileen invited me to play some sort of scavenger hunt? I buzzed once. No answer. I was about to turn and walk away when I noticed that the lock to the building's inner door hadn't quite caught. I pushed the door open and walked down the hallway — its warped walls covered in countless layers of industrial gray paint — to apartment 3 at the back of the building. I knocked steadily. Nothing. A wad of papers had been jammed between the door and the frame near the knob. I assumed they were those ubiquitous menus for takeout Chinese food that were thrust in doorways across the city. I was about to walk away when something caught my eye. I plucked one of the leaflets from the pile, sending the others scattering across the heavily scuffed floor.

The flyer—illustrated with what looked like an African batik print of a turbaned figure in a lotus position crowned with a crescent and a star—advertised the services of an African mystic in Tottenville, Staten Island who specialized in "Palmistry, Tarot, and the ancient African ritual of Naarem." I immediately looked around to see if someone was watching me. Surely, this couldn't have been a coincidence.

Heading back to the subway, I made sure to pass by the funeral parlor where I'd seen Issa. A group of African men and women in traditional African fabrics embroidered with colorful accents were greeting each other solemnly in front, offering condolences in their native tongue, whatever that may have been. The language had a heavily grounded cadence and rhythm, not unlike the drums that formed a soundtrack to Western depictions of African ritual and culture.

There were several men as tall as Issa in the crowd, and while scanning their faces to find my coworker from the restaurant, I nearly walked right into Brad.

"Glen!"

"Brad. Sorry. I was lost in my own thoughts."

"I heard about your mom."

"How?"

"Carl told me. Are you okay?"

"Yeah, I guess so." I couldn't help but notice his black suit and tie, a far cry from the torn jeans he wore to class or even the white shirt and burgundy tie that was our uniform at the restaurant.

"If there's anything I can do…"

"No, I'm fine." I glanced beyond him to the crowd still emerging from the funeral parlor. "Looks like someone important must have died."

"Oh, I think that's just a typical African funeral."

I waited for him to continue, expecting him to explain his connection to all this.

"Or so I've heard." He looked nervous, like I'd caught him at something. He glanced into the crowd as if searching for a familiar face, then looked at his watch. "Crap. I've got to go. When are you leaving for Chicago?"

"In less than a week."

"Look, call me if there's anything I can do, okay?"

"Sure."

I watched him as he darted off down 4th, zigzagging through honking taxis, in the direction of the museum. My eyes happened to move back to the crowd in front of the funeral parlor where they caught Issa standing in the doorway, separated from me by rows of other mourners. His eyes locked into mine, never blinking as he watched me. He only smiled, fixing his gaze on me till I was jostled out of his sight by people passing by. When I looked back, he had disappeared in the crowd.

Invisible.

I thought I could feel the weight of someone's stare following me as I descended into the subway, but scanning the faces of the people around me and across the platform, I found their eyes either buried in books or studying the unspeakably filthy crannies between the rails of the subway below. There was nothing wrong with Brad accompanying Issa to a memorial service for a friend or family member, I told myself. But I couldn't shake the eerie feeling I had. Why be so secretive about it? And since when had Brad been such a friend of the African brothers at the restaurant? Anyway, what was the thing Issa had passed him?

None of this was my business, I decided, once the number 6 had whisked me away. I looked into my backpack for something to read and found the flyer about the medium. I pulled out my bus map of Staten Island. Tottenville was on the extreme southwestern tip of the island, fourteen miles from the St. George ferry terminal, or a little more than the distance from one tip of Manhattan to the other. It might be a wild goose chase, but it couldn't hurt to check it out.

12 a.m.

Back at home, there was no message from Eileen. If only I'd asked for her number. Now I would have to stop by the museum again. What if she'd been merely leading me on? But I couldn't believe that. Not after the way she'd laughed when she'd spoken to me.

I tried to recall her image. There'd been something almost wild in those dark eyes as she spoke of the home she'd fallen in love with. Her mouth had been firm yet somehow voluptuous — ripe as a wound. I'd studied her tiny white hand resting on the banister at the top of the main staircase — the fingers had been small and delicate, with neatly clipped nails. She hadn't been wearing nail polish or rings. I hadn't noticed any makeup either. Her skin was firm and completely clear, a perfectly clean background on which her deep black eyes rested like crisp bold text on a blank page.

A vision.

I did a search for Café Angelico online. As it turns out, there used to be one about three years ago at 74 East 3rd Street — where the Internet Café is today. So, I guess she'd been referring it by its old name and got the address wrong. I probably hadn't waited long enough for her. End of the mystery.

Just as I was processing the implications of this, the phone rang.

"Hello, Glen?"

"Eileen?"

"Yes!"

"I couldn't find you."

"I know, I'm so sorry about that. I tried calling to cancel, but we had a record number of visitors at the museum, and I ended up working straight through my shift. Can you let me make it up to you?"

After rescheduling, I should have been happy. It wasn't her fault and she'd called to cancel, after all. But something was still eating away at me.

Another direction.

I was sure I would see Eileen again, but somehow I knew that the major intersection of our destinies had run its course. There was no shaking the gnawing sense of disappointment that washed over me.

I was about to shut down my computer, when I remembered Issa's face in the doorway of the funeral parlor. As I'd left the restaurant the other day, I'd meant to ask his brother if either of them had ever heard of the Naarem.

I pulled out *The African Origins of the Tarot.* Where had Ouédrago done his research again? Among the Lobi people. A search for the Lobi turned up the name of the country where the Lobi resided: Burkina Faso.

No accidents.

I would have to go back to the restaurant and ask them about this. Why hadn't they shared more when they knew the subject of my research? And why had Issa avoided me today in the crowd?

I decided to do a reading to clear my thoughts. The more I study the cards, the harder I need to work to listen to the stories they are capable of telling. To experience their mystery and wonder now, I must discipline myself to concentrate. Is this the price of knowledge, or have I simply become numb?

Searching for a question, I thought of asking about my work, but that was clearly not the subject dominating my concerns. Besides, that would have been like asking the cards about themselves. As I shuffled in search of a subject, Eileen's laughter kept rising to the surface of my consciousness. I'd been drawn to her by her physical beauty, so maybe the cerebral connection I'd begun to feel for her was nothing but a projection of my fantasy onto her.

The Moon card popped up again, but this time in position one. Of course. It was so obvious now. The Moon was Eileen, not my mother. My deepest fears and suspicions about Eileen were confirmed in the story told by the cards. I was allowing myself to be charmed too easily. One surprise, though, was a large number of Staves, suggesting a period of great creativity approaching. Maybe I could get back on track with my work. But again, the upcoming travels were rapidly approaching, and while that could represent my trip to Chicago, I began seeing a pattern of a larger journey looming on the horizon.

You must let go to follow.

It had been a long time since I'd done such an intensive reading, and I left it feeling frustrated. Had I merely read my own aimlessness into the cards and not been receptive enough to new answers? That I needed to ask at all gave me my answer, but I didn't know how to try any harder.

Not that I believed a single reading could ever unlock all the answers, but in the past I'd always been able to uncover some aspect of my situation that hadn't occurred to me until I'd noticed it in the cards. The cards' rich symbolism illustrates virtually every state a human being is capable of reaching over the course of a lifetime, and whether one is aware of it or not, all those possible states coexist simultaneously, somewhere deep inside a person. Whether viewed as a game or the remnants of an ancient ritual, the cards remind the reader about those states of awareness that have drifted back into the unconscious. In reminding us about our dormant emotions and experiences, the cards offer us new possibilities.

Take the journey.

It's just that ever since I began turning my examination of the cards into a scholarly pursuit, I'm having more and more trouble recognizing the possibilities. Each new reading seems more confused and directionless than the last. I no longer know which direction to go.

I lay awake in my bed looking out at the Manhattan skyline, thinking of how I had come to the point where my mind was so limited in what it could allow itself to see.

Then I thought of my mother. In worrying about everything else, I'd allowed myself to put her out of my mind again. Each time my thoughts return to her in the hospital bed, I feel nauseous, as if the floor has been pulled from under me and I'm falling.

Follow.

I picked up the phone to call my dad, but suddenly conscious of the hour, I hung up before letting the phone ring. I went to sleep determined to find a destination in my dreams of those infinite corridors.

Chapter Seven

THE HIEROPHANT

Ritualism, ceremonies. Mercy, kindness, forgiveness. Timid captivity to one's own ideas. A person with a sense of religious and historical importance.

A tremendous robe hangs from his broad, majestic form. The billowing garment, which covers the arms of the throne in which the old man is firmly planted, is adorned with rows of golden hexagons, each framed in a deep blue circle and etched with a series of thin lines fanning out from the center where they twist together. He is hunched forward, but his large, clear eyes stare knowingly from above his long white beard, suggesting that his slouching posture is more the physical result of his advanced age than his mental resignation to it. On his head sits a gilded, three-tiered hat, inscribed with curious white symbols. His arms part the robe, and its lush green lining stands in stark contrast with the blousy white garment he wears next to his skin. He holds up one hand, extending three fingers in what could very well be a ritualistic blessing. His other hand balances a scepter, which rests on the ground beside his throne. A large golden cross at the top of this staff is barely visible, all but disappearing into the golden background, as if into a secret world visible only to those as well-initiated as he is.

October 23, 8:15 a.m.

I went to terrible new places in my dream last night. Heaping hospital beds rolled past me at a frightening speed as I ran in the other direction. There were no nurses or doctors pushing these phantom gurneys, so I was horrified to think what lay beneath their white sheets, penned in by those silver hospital bars. The pounding soundtrack of the dream was drowned out for a moment with the squeaking of so many wheels rolling over endless hospital hallways past countless doors. Behind one of them, my mother lay in unspeakable pain, crying out for me, but I couldn't find her anywhere. And then everything began falling away as I jerked awake into a cold sweat.

October 23, 9:30 p.m.

Today I finally found the key to moving on with my life and my work. It was a day of many lessons. I called Dad as soon as I was up, seeing my dream as a sign I should be with him in Chicago. He was just on his way to the hospital.

"I'll be taking her home any day now."

"I should be there."

"It will be better when she's back home. Right now, she's just sleeping a lot. Sometimes she kicks me out of her room when I'm there. She's trying to be brave."

"But she doesn't have to be."

"I've told her it's okay to be afraid, but then she just changes the subject, asking me if the food in the hospital's cafeteria is any good."

"So she's better."

"Call her and see for yourself."

"But what if she's sleeping?"

"She's on morphine, so it's not like you'll disturb her for long, and I'll be waking her up when I get there in a half-hour."

I paced around the apartment a bit before I was able to work up the nerve to push the buttons on the phone. I kept thinking of those mourners in front of the funeral parlor the day before. They had seemed so brave in the face of death, huddled together to confront their loved one's passing with proud resignation.

Let it be.

I took a deep breath and called Mom. She sounded a bit groggy, but her complaints about the nurses' poking and prodding showed that at least a bit of her personality had returned.

"You must be in horrible pain," I said, feeling stupid as the useless sentence rolled from my tongue.

"It's bad," she sighed. "But I'll be all right. You'll be here when I get out this week, right?"

"Yep. My flight is in a couple of days. But I can come right away..."

"No, no. Wait till I'm out of here. There's nothing you can do. How are your studies coming along?" I could hear in the way she exhaled her sentences — meting them out in slightly trembling little fragments — that she was more scared then she wanted to let on. But by asking me about my studies, I got the idea that what she needed more than anything right now was to believe she wasn't interfering with my life. I had to pretend to care more about myself right now to make her feel like everything was okay.

"I've been busy researching my thesis," I said, adding a few more vague words about the advances I'd made without troubling her with the actual questions and doubts that have been plaguing me.

"Oh, that's wonderful. You've already done so much more than the average person has in a lifetime."

This wasn't the kind of thing my mother would have said. It was as if she were preparing to say goodbye. Her voice had become so faint, as if she had slipped away one more layer from the living. Was she giving up?

Get ready for the journey.

As I spoke to her, I struggled to sound normal, but when the distance and futility of the call became unbearable, I said I'd see her in a few days and hung up.

After that, there was no way in hell I was going to be able to concentrate on homework. The flyer I'd found yesterday in the East Village lay on the floor near my backpack where I must have dropped it the night before. I would check it out.

I caught the Staten Island Railroad to Tottenville, a trip that took much longer than I'd anticipated. Never had it occurred to me that New York's most forgotten borough was actually bigger than Manhattan. On the New York City subway map, after all, it has been made much smaller to fit into the same rectangle with the rest of the city. There is a warning about the map not being drawn to scale, but the diminutive Staten Island plastered across subway posters all over town is the only image of the place most New Yorkers have, thereby shrinking the place in the city's collective consciousness.

On the train — from which there was precious little to see — I thumbed through *The African Origins of the Tarot*, giving a closer read to the first two chapters. The word "Naarem," Ouédrago says, originated from an old African word for "soul searching," though he never mentions which African language this word supposedly came from. Why the omission of such facts? And why not mention that the Lobi people lived in what is currently called Burkina Faso?

Truth is beyond any language.

I suspected that it was simply the author's avoidance of any colonizer's references in describing Africa that kept him from referring to names of modern African states, preferring to speak of kingdoms and ethnic groups whose origins dated from many centuries ago rather than giving credibility to borders that had been arbitrarily imposed by European invaders. But this approach hardly made his work accessible to readers outside Africa.

When I got off at Tottenville, I felt like I was at the other end of the earth, not the other end of the island. As I wandered around the eerily deserted streets of the neighborhood, I found it difficult to believe that in its glory days Tottenville had been a bustling town, one of the Island's first, built long before bridges and ferries had connected the island to New York City. Along Main Street, a smattering of historic buildings gave the sense of an evacuated coastal town in England, Holland, or Denmark. But no, none of those places felt quite like this — like a word on the tip of your tongue that can never quite be retrieved.

A corner bodega with a few faded packages in the window was the only business that appeared to be open. I bought a soda there from an overweight Italian teenager with a thick New York accent and drooping eyelids, and sipped it as I strolled down a side street to Conference House park.

As I walked through the multicolored autumn leaves scattered across lawn around the historic stone building, I looked over the strip of water separating New York from New Jersey — a postcard-perfect picture with no one but me to enjoy it.

I set off, anxious to find the mystic advertised on the flyer. According to my map, Surf Avenue could be just as easily reached along the coast as by the paved inland roads, so I bundled my jacket tightly against the autumn wind and took to the sand. Unlike the cluttered golden beaches closer to Manhattan, Tottenville's stretch of coastline has a strange rugged beauty, with bits of washed-up seaweed, shells, rocks, and the occasional piece of trash. The skeleton of a burnt-out pickup truck sat rusting in the crook of a sharp curve of white sand. But elements of nature constantly reasserted themselves against man's hostile influence, slowly feeding off the edges of the metropolis to suck the city back into a brackish, watery grave. Humanity's hold on the planet was tenuous at best, even here in New York.

You will find the right balance.

Finding a path back to the inland streets, I wound up directly on Surf Avenue, where a series of homes — not much more than shacks, really — were hidden from the street in a tangle of trees and bushes. Junked auto parts littered the lawns. I could easily have been in some backwater town in the Deep South rather than in New York. Would some mad hillbilly suddenly emerge on his front porch with a shotgun?

And then, I realized it was one of these ramshackle dwellings that bore the address listed on the flyer. To summon my courage, I reminded myself I was less than a two-hour commute from Times Square, and approached the door. The place was just a little wooden cottage — its screened front porch about ready to crack off from the main structure. A small plaque on the porch door announced, "Botu Mosabwe. African Seer. By Appointment Only." Topping the sign was the same crescent and star design from the flyer, hand-painted in red, yellow, and green, the colors of Africa.

From beyond the front door I heard movement, then a young child's cry, followed immediately by an adult's irritated shout and the sudden clattering of what might have been pots and pans. I debated whether it might be better to come back another time, but then thought of the long commute, and figured I'd better get this over and done with. I rapped sharply on the screen door. The clatter inside immediately subsided, and a moment later I heard footsteps approaching. I imagined them amplified to the level of the stomping in my recurring nightmare.

Listen.

The sound of a door being unlatched snapped me from my reveries, and a woman — who I presumed was Botu Mosabwe herself — peered out onto the front porch. She frowned at me through the screen door. "Can I help you?"

"I… Yes. Well, I think so. I found your flyer, and I had a question I thought you could…"

"I charge $30 for half-hour sessions and $50 for the full hour." She leaned on the inside of the front door to keep it open as she rolled up the sleeves on her oversized embroidered shirt, tailored from a bolt of deep green fabric.

"Oh, I wasn't looking for a reading. I'm actually studying the Tarot, and…"

"I don't read Tarot cards, and I don't give lessons to psychics." Her accent was clearly American, not African. She made no movement from the door, and the awkwardness of addressing her through the porch screen was making me uncomfortable.

"No, I wasn't looking for that sort of thing either. It's the Naarem mentioned on your flyer that interested me."

"As I said, it's $30 for the half-hour."

Though I hadn't come for a reading, or whatever it was she called it, that seemed the only way she would be willing to communicate. At the end I could see if there was any way to win her over enough to tell me something of what she knew about the African history of the cards. "Can I start with a half-hour?"

"Fine. Can you come back next week…"

"Oh, well, I live on the other end of the island, and I was hoping you could see me now."

"Why were you in such a hurry to come and see me, if it's so out of your way?" she snapped.

The suddenness of her challenge demanded an answer, and I found myself feeling a need to justify myself. "You mentioned Naarem, which corresponds to a reference in my studies…"

"So you're interested in African culture, huh?" She stepped out onto the porch, letting the front door to her house swing shut behind her. Walking up to the inside of the porch door, she gave me a penetrating stare through the screen.

"Yes." I nodded.

"Come in," she said, unlatching the outer door and waving me through the porch into her house. Inside, the sent of incense was almost overpowering. "What is your name?"

"Glen."

"Botu." She scooped up a wailing baby from a basket near the door, popping a pacifier in its mouth with the seamless gesture of an experienced mother. An earthy glow permeated the room, originating from the colors of African fabrics draped over lampshades around the living room. Soon the baby quieted down, and she invited me to squat on a woven mat in the center of the room, just between the television (which she turned off) and the sofa (a faux-leather job in an earth-toned shell print). "How did you find my flyer?"

"I…" It was hard to get into the details of the discovery without embarrassing myself. "A friend," I simplified.

"A *new* friend," she said knowingly. "And why Naarem?"

"I heard it spoken of in *The African Origins of the Tarot*," I braved.

Her eyebrows arched at my reference, and her wide dark eyes seemed to dilate ever so slightly. I noticed that she had beautifully smooth skin, though her eyes betrayed a more advanced age. The child was surely not her own — probably a grandchild. There were gray streaks running through her perfectly rounded Afro. She removed a large rectangular box from beneath her sofa. It was covered with hand-tooled leather. Noticing my interest in it, she leaned forward, and said softly, "From Mali."

Everything about her softened once she began her work. Her gestures became broad and flowing, her breath slow and steady. Removing the cover of the box, she pulled out a stack of well-worn rectangular cards. "Naarem," she said, then asked me to think of a question as she shuffled the deck. Unlike the cards Ouédrago had described, hers had been printed on glossy card stock by a modern publisher and were decorated with scenes from everyday life in Africa. "Don't look at the images," she said patiently. "Let your mind's eye guide you on the question."

Of course, my question was about the cards themselves, since that's what I'd come for. Botu's cards were nothing more than a manufactured deck of 78 Tarot cards illustrated with printed reproductions of naïve art with an African flavor. Her method of laying them out was an only slightly modified interpretation of the Celtic Cross so popular among Tarot readers.

Not that there was anything inherently wrong in any of this, but it was becoming clear that I'd learn little about Ouédrago's "original" African cards from Botu. Oddly enough, the reading itself confirmed the futility of finding more. After a series of missed starts ("You may be falling out of love with someone... No, it's more a changing of careers..."), she finally concluded, "You have a great barrier to cross in reaching your current goals. The answers you are searching for are not so apparent. Look not in the physical to find what you can only gather from within the soul."

Discouraged by these vague interpretations, I figured I had nothing to lose in asking her about the Ouédrago text, but as I prepared to speak, suddenly she looked up from the cards and directly into my eyes.

"Pull another card from the deck," she said.

I selected a card and turned it over. It was a single male youth... a knight or page? With an African mortar and pestle. Was this the equivalent of a stave in Botu's deck? Across the figure's face was an earthen smudge.

"It's no accident that you found your way here," she said. "At first I thought so, but now I know you were meant to come."

The card was exactly like the card from Italy I'd seen at the library, the Page of Staves with the ocher stain across the surface. I reached out to touch it, but already her hand was advancing towards the cards, which she scooped up in a single motion to return them to the deck.

"Look not in the physical," she said, looking directly into my eyes again. "Your most important lessons will never be found there."

"That card..."

"How did you find me?"

"Your flyer," I explained, still trying to process what I had seen. "I found one in the East Village."

"Yes. My daughter and I brought them to all the New Yorkers who had attended the Afro-Caribbean book fair last spring."

"You delivered them yourself?"

"Across the five boroughs."

"Why not mail them?"

"It is not the African way to be so distant. We visit each of our people individually. That's the only way the job can be done."

Well, printing out flyers probably wasn't the true African way either, I thought, but whatever gets the customers coming to the far end of Staten Island. Why didn't she want me to see that card?

"You are afraid of what you can't see," she said with a confident laugh as if she'd read my thoughts.

"Maybe we all are at a certain level," I said. "But I'm fascinated by your deck. I've never seen one like it."

"Look not in the physical," she lectured. Then softly, almost pleadingly, she added, "Do you have time to stay for another exercise?"

"Well, I hadn't prepared to…"

"There's no additional charge," she implored. "It's important."

I dared not say no, even though I was beginning to feel a bit claustrophobic under her intense gaze.

"Close your eyes and pick an object," she said, holding out a jelly jar full of pebbles, shells, and other bits of what looked like debris collected at the nearby beach.

Not wanting to stick my hand too far in, fearful of what I might find, I aimed for something on the surface.

"Don't be afraid," she said. "There's nothing that can hurt you but your own fear."

Fair enough, I thought as I dug down beyond what felt like twigs and stones and shells and bits of hair. I grabbed onto something smooth — possibly a coin or button. I opened my eyes as I pulled it out of the jar. It was a small polished silver stone.

"Hold it up to the light," she said.

With the light shining through, it became transparent and lavender, then back on the floor it was silver again as the light bounced off, not through it.

"Invisibility," she said. "You are in a benign conjunction with the Sun and the Moon. Your color is trapped inside. The light eludes you."

I waited for more, as she picked up the stone and dropped it back in the jar, returning it with the box of cards to a cabinet near the television. She saw I was waiting. "Oh, that's all," she said. "I think we've accomplished a lot for one day."

"Yes." I was a bit disoriented, suddenly. I'd almost forgotten what I'd come for. Was I truly invisible? Then I remembered my question. "Botu… I wondered where the word Naarem comes from."

"You said you had read *The African Origins of the Tarot* so you must know the answer."

"Do you know the book? Is that where you heard of the word?"

Laughing, she got up from the mat as if to indicate our time was definitely finished. "You're so literal — always looking for a label to pin on things."

"So you haven't heard of the book, then."

Her laughter turned to a scowl. "I told you when you arrived: I don't read Tarot." She stood between me and the door. I crossed the front porch, turning on the stairs to say, "I'm sorry, I didn't mean to…"

"Remember, the light is missing you," she said as she snapped the screen door shut in my face. Before I could say goodbye, she had crossed the porch and shut herself behind the front door again. The cry of the baby resumed as if on cue.

Already it was growing dark, and I was freezing. I made my way quickly back to Main Street. The streets remained virtually deserted, though there were a few lights in some of the weathered homes along the way. The odd car passed through. The shop where I'd purchased the soda was shut. Before reaching the Staten Island Railroad stop, I came upon a parked bus. Its stocky driver was just firing up the engine.

"Where do you go?" I asked.

"'Da ferry," he said a thick Italian-American New York accent. I hopped on and moved all the way to the back. His hairy forearm threw a lever, the doors closed with a hiss, and we were off.

I tried reading for a while, but the bus shook too much, and I think I was still a bit rattled by the visit to the African mystic. That ocher color across the face in the card…it couldn't have been an accident, especially with her so eager to cover it. But why? And thinking of the Page of Staves reminded me that I would have to get in touch with Dr. Carter to find out if he'd called his contact at the Morgan Library to ask about testing the card. Had he just said he'd do that to get me out of his office?

Don't look in the physical.

What if there was something to what Botu said? Was I not seeing what was around me? What if I was making myself invisible by not allowing the light or truth to enter?

Gazing out the window of the bus, I caught sight of the strange silhouettes of shipwrecks off the western shore of the island. I'd read about these but had no idea how isolated the area was, or how haunting these rusted carcasses were, half-submerged in Arthur Kill, the shallow tidal strait that separates Staten Island from New Jersey. A strange flash of déjà vu washed over me, just as the wrecks disappeared between the trees in the distance. I looked back up to the front of the bus and happened to catch the driver's eyes in his rearview mirror. *Creepy, huh?* his stare seemed to say.

When I finally got home, I realized that once again I'd spent an entire day following hunches and accomplishing nothing. Why am I drifting this way?

Soon you will hear.

October 24, 12:30 a.m.

I read my cards for hours, searching for a new direction. They kept suggesting that a powerful creative force is steering me.

So why couldn't I feel it?

I thought about what Botu had said about me not allowing the light to enter. What exactly did she mean? I've been receptive to every signal that has been sent my way, haven't I? I've followed every sign, studied every symbol, analyzed every thought...

Soon I'll be back in Chicago with Mom and Dad again. If only I could be truly certain of my purpose in life when I get there — as sure of it as the cards are sure about each story they tell — then Mom could go ahead and...

But, no, it can't be her time yet! I just don't see the signs pointing that way right now, and I mustn't will it into being.

Let things be as they are.

And that's when it hit me with complete clarity: Maybe I've been so focused on *doing* something that I haven't really allowed myself to understand how things *are*. I can still follow my instincts, but instead of trying to predict the path before following it, maybe I'll be better off just experiencing everything completely. I don't need to try to make things fit into a thesis or prove anything to anyone. If academics can't allow themselves to see the power in the Tarot, I don't need to show them. They can tell their own story. But I need to listen to the story the cards are telling me instead of trying to write my own.

From now on, I will let the light enter.

Chapter Eight

EIGHT OF STAVES

Sudden, rapid advancement. Hastily made decisions. Events moving too quickly.

The eight slender objects are arranged into two symmetrical groups, each made of four long, parallel rods staggered slightly like steps. These two groups are set over one another — like four fingers of one hand resting across the four identical digits of the other — to form a completely symmetrical diamond at the sixteen sparkling points where they intersect. Unlike fingers, however, these objects have no corporal attachment. Nor is it possible to tell from their flatness which group rests on the surface and which lies in the background. They would be little more than criss-crossing lines were each not decorated with two great golden knobs, one at either end. There are sixteen of these urn-like ornaments in all, drawing the viewer's eye outward to what lies beyond in every direction.

October 24, 4:30 p.m.

Another day of discoveries and revelations. I woke this morning from a dream of a secret meeting in a distant place that resembled the far end of Staten Island, except in my dream version of the setting, the paths and tangles of trees seemed infinite. Just when I thought I was lost, I found myself in a the long hallway from my recurring nightmare. A woman was behind one of the doors in the infinite corridor.

It was Eileen from the museum. She didn't say a word but took my face in her hands and kissed me…

The dream faded into a deep wave of sadness as I woke to thoughts of my mother in her hospital bed, surrounded by the tubes of so many machines. I had to shake the image out of my head and get on with things. I'd be seeing her in a few days, and it didn't do me any good to torture myself by worrying.

Let the light enter.

Eileen. It was Sunday today. That was the day of the training at the Trader's House. But it was already 10:30. It was so gray and dreary out. Still, if I caught the 11 a.m. ferry, I'd be just in time to get there by noon. It would be just the thing to clear my mind…

After a quick shower, I ran down the hill past Borough Hall, then down the ramp into the ferry terminal, and managed to make it onto the boat just as the attendant was detaching the ropes from the dock.

I stared across the dark harbor at the immense steel and glass structures poking up from Manhattan as if directly out of the depths of the sea. To think that when the Trader's Home had been built, Staten Island had just begun to serve as a resort for those who'd made their new fortunes in New York.

Since that time, the transportation between the islands had barely changed. The boat still creaked slowly into the landing in lower Manhattan, banging and squeaking against the giant wooden fender piles. The attendants still parted the rickety old metal gates by hand, allowing the passengers to descend upon the other, more slender island, where they ventured down into one of the world's oldest underground transportation systems.

I'm sure I looked a bit disheveled when I arrived at the museum, but Eileen beamed when she found me at the front door. "You've decided to join us! That's great." She seemed anxious to play her part to the fullest today, buttoned up in a lacy white blouse with ruffled sleeves. Her black pleated skirt and jacket were as grim as the weather, serving only to make her soft, white skin more beautiful by contrast. "I'm sorry about the other day."

"No worries."

"I'm just glad you made it." She escorted me into the parlor. "Isn't this room just lovely?" she asked with a sigh, as if noticing it for the first time.

"It really is." Looking up at the Greek revival accents bordering the ceiling, my eyes scanned downward past the beveled mirrors above the colonnaded fireplace to the Romanesque prints on the brightly colored carpeting.

"Here let me take your coat. By the way, I asked Grace about the reference to those cards on our site, and she said…" The front door creaked open, and a stylishly dressed woman of about fifty entered the room. "Here's Grace now! Grace, this is Glen. He's here to attend the training today."

"Oh, wonderful," she said shaking my hand with only the slightest pressure, as if I were another piece of porcelain being inspected and tagged for acquisition. "We're always happy to have another history lover join our family of volunteers. I hear you're a student of history."

"Art history, actually."

"Oh, what area?"

"The Tarocchi," I said, hoping the Italian name would lend a touch of authority.

"Yes, Eileen mentioned your interest in those cards."

"The Naarem, or 'Nared,' as your site says."

"I'm embarrassed to admit our site is so outdated. The content was hastily compiled by my predecessor in an effort to get something up and running, but we need to completely revamp it. Perhaps this could be an area of interest for you."

"Yes, that would be fascinating. Do you happen to know anything about where that reference to 'Nared' came from?"

"In our training today, we'll discuss what we actually know about the house and its former inhabitants and what is merely hearsay."

She spoke with an icy precision, sidestepping my question like a politician, as if I'd taken an enormously inappropriate liberty.

There are those who don't allow themselves to hear.

Another knock at the door heralded the entrance of a middle-aged man wearing a button-down shirt with an oversized navy tie and a pair of wire spectacles. "Welcome, Ben," said Grace, taking his raincoat, which was beaded with drops. "It must have started pouring the moment the rest of us set foot in the door. Unfortunately, you weren't as lucky in avoiding the downpour, were you?"

"Yes, it certainly is coming down out there. What a perfect day to spend in this home, though, don't you think? I find the sound of the rain and thunder make it easier to imagine the past."

"Ben, this is Glen," said Eileen, introducing us.

Ben dried off his glasses with a tissue and held out his hand to me. "Pleasure."

"Good to meet you," I said, returning the shake. His hand was thin and papery.

"What brings you to volunteer as a docent?" he inquired.

"I'm completing a degree in art history, and I was inspired by a recent visit."

"I'm a retired history professor myself." His eyes rounded with curiosity. "Where are you studying?"

"City University of New York."

"Oh, well, I was at Brooklyn College, which is part of CUNY. Perhaps I know your professors."

"Well, my main advisor is Dr. Carter, who…"

"By any chance could that be Dr. Elliott Carter?"

"Yes."

"What a coincidence! He just phoned me the other day about an artifact he'd discovered."

Listen.

I would definitely need to call Carter to see if he'd contacted the Morgan Library about the Italian card. Surely, that couldn't be the artifact Ben was talking about — he'd never mentioned the library.

But before I could formulate a question, Grace was asking us to take one of the folding chairs that had been set up in the main parlor for the orientation. "Welcome to our historic home and museum. As you know, my name is Grace Collingsworth, and I'm the volunteer coordinator…"

She launched into the walking tour Eileen had given me a few days earlier. Grace knew we'd already been through this information once and that the training manuals left on our seats covered the same information in even greater detail, so her didactic repetition of the information seemed mostly to reinforce her own sense of importance. She was delighted to have a captive subordinate audience.

"Now, as you talk about the objects in the kitchen, be sure and mention the pie cooler. As you will see from the materials in your manual, it was designed to keep out insects and possibly the servants." She giggled quietly over this last observation as if savoring a dirty joke. "If asked *when* the pie cooler was brought into the house, we say, 'around the middle of the 19th century.' That usually covers us on any pieces in the collection for which we don't have exact dates, and it sounds much more authoritative than 'I don't know.'" She raised her finger to her nose in a "shhhh" gesture as if she'd just handed over one of the great secrets of the old house.

"Most people don't ask for more precise dates," confirmed Eileen. "I find they really are here to be told a story."

"Which is not to say that we are exempt from memorizing the precise information we do posses," returned Grace. "It's important to know which pieces are original to the family who lived here, and which have been acquired from other collections."

My mind wandered from Grace's presentation as I studied the spines of the worn volumes on the shelves behind her. Did any hold information on the Tarot, I wondered? I imagined the sisters who'd lived in the house picking through these same books in search of one to capture their imaginations. They must have read by candlelight in the early days before the gas fixtures were installed.

It was almost impossible to imagine them without investing the scenario with the usual clichés. "Shall we have our tea in the parlor, sister dear?" It couldn't really have been like that, could it? But what *had* it been like?

Ben and Eileen were folding up chairs, so I followed their example. Grace led us upstairs, past the restored bedrooms on the second floor to the third.

"This floor is not open to visitors," said Grace. "It would have originally been the children's rooms. However, as the sisters lived here alone towards the end, they kept these rooms purely for storage, which is why none of the original furnishings remain. Today, this is where we keep the smaller objects — letters, garments, jewelry, cutlery, etc. — that haven't yet found a home in the rooms open to public viewing. We're cataloging everything piece by piece, which, as I'm sure you can imagine, is an extremely laborious process."

Spread out on a large folding table was a pair of petticoats. "I sometimes wonder what the sisters would think if they knew we were restoring their underwear," Grace remarked with a naughty laugh. I got the distinct impression that she only permitted such improprieties if *she* proposed them. "I've been trying to duplicate the stitch on that one there, and it's painstaking work. Imagine the sisters doing all that work on hundreds of garments — all by themselves!" There was something almost morbid in her fascination with the details of these faded objects. It was as if she wanted to revive the sisters or become one of them.

"Over here we have all the documents they left behind," said Grace, turning our attention to a stack of boxes that stood waist high and ran the length of one wall. "There are hundreds of letters, as well as an assortment of bills, deeds, receipts, and other papers. As we catalog them, we're constantly uncovering fascinating little glimpses into the sisters' daily life, which, eventually, I'll condense into my history of the house."

"That's going to be an enormous undertaking," said Ben. "If there's any way in which I can be of help, please let me know." He was nearly drooling over the documents as he compared notes with her on their different areas of expertise. "I'm particularly fascinated in the evolution of decorative furnishings in the mid-nineteenth century," he mentioned at one point, going into rhapsodies over the horsehair divan in the parlor. Grace, on the other hand, was mostly concerned with the social and domestic life of the sisters. Surely, I thought, they'd be able to use each other to further their own agendas without entering into any sort of competition.

My research topic couldn't represent much of a threat either, I figured, so I braved a question. "In what you've seen so far, have you run across anything on the parlor games played in the house?"

"Oh, there are a number of references to parlor games."

"Anything involving Tarot readings or any sort of fortune telling?"

Grace prickled. "Not that I've come across, though many of our visitors certainly like to hear stories of the ghosts some have suggested are flying about the place." She shot a smile to Ben as if to say not all volunteer candidates were as literate as he.

"I didn't mean to suggest that supernatural forces were at work here or anything like that," I countered. "I was simply interested to know if the inhabitants of the home played games of divination — even if they were played for sheer entertainment." It came out sarcastic, and Grace was clearly not amused. I may have been a volunteer and not a paid employee, but she was still the boss.

You haven't learned to listen.

"No, I haven't come across any evidence of such games, though I'll be sure and let you know if I do." She turned to lead us down the stairs, followed by Ben, then Eileen, who lingered a step behind to catch me away from the others.

"Grace can be a bit intense, but once you're in, you're going to love giving tours here."

"Yes, this might be just the thing for me," I said, the words escaping me before I realized how far from the truth they were. Her eyes were locked on mine and her cheeks were flushed. It was as if she were one of the sisters, waiting alone in the house for a suitor to plant a kiss. I was in danger of doing just that, and Grace certainly wouldn't have approved, so I looked down to break her hypnotic stare.

My glance settled on the bottom row of boxes, where the light reflected off something. It was a scrap of paper no bigger than a dime — a tiny rounded corner torn from a larger piece. "It should be exciting," I said, looking back at Eileen before her eyes had a chance to follow mine to the ground. "Looks like we're getting left behind."

"Oh!" She dashed ahead to catch up. Finding myself alone for a moment, I acted before thinking, grabbed the errant bit of paper and swept it into my pocket. I could feel its thickness — like that of an old photo.

A sign.

It was pouring as I left the house to run down into the subway. Once settled into my seat, I glanced around to be sure I was being ignored by the other passengers in classic New York style. I pulled the stiff, brittle scrap of paper from my pocket and studied it. One side was a deep red, not an earthy ocher like the smudge on the Page of Staves but a clouded ruby color like the backs of the cards in the Visconti-Sforza deck. The other side had a few lines of deep green and gold. From the tiny, faded brush strokes, it was obvious the paint had been applied by a person, not a machine, probably many years ago.

I would have to work my way into the favors of Grace by working as a volunteer so I would be able to search the artifacts for the rest of the card — maybe I'd even find a complete deck.

Look beyond the physical.

I placed the torn paper between the pages of the docent training manual and continued on to the university to see Dr. Carter.

But it was Sunday, I realized, and Carter wouldn't be there.

At 23rd Street, I got out to turn around and head back home. Coming up the stairs to cross to the other platform, I bumped right into Salif.

"Hey, Salif!"

"Monsieur Glen."

"I was thinking of you," I found myself saying.

"Me?"

"You told me about magic. And you gave me that card…"

"Ah yes, you're playing with the cards in school." He made a sound like laughter, but his eyes remained fixed on me, deadly serious.

"I wondered if you'd ever heard of the Naarem. I think they might be from Burkina Faso."

"Maybe no one knows where they're from."

"But have you ever heard of them?"

"I've heard a lot of things. That you left the restaurant because your mother is very ill. And now you are here. Why don't you go home to her?"

"I…" And all my reasons crumbled away. My mother was dying, and I wasn't at her side.

"Go to her."

I nodded to him and descended the stairs to the downtown trains. As I waited for the doors to part, I saw him staring me from the other platform, his mouth a flat line, his eyes impenetrable.

That look has stayed with me all the way home, while I wrote in my journal, as if he has been watching me the entire time.

7:45 p.m.

At home, there were eleven messages on my machine.

Dad had called to say Mom was in a lot of pain and that it was a good thing I was coming in a few days. I'd already decided I would move my flight up to tomorrow, and this only confirmed it. That stare Salif had fixed on me…not that it mattered now. I just had to go to her.

Be where you must be.

But first the other messages. There were a number of hang-ups, followed by an out-of-breath Dr. Carter. "Glen, I'm sure you're with your family, but I wanted to let you know I didn't drop the ball. I called my colleague at the Morgan Library, and it seems the card you were shown — the one flown in from that town outside Milan — well, it's gone missing. What's especially strange is that the collector who requested it be flown in — a Mr. Waydren? Waydrag? — can't be located. This is all being kept confidential, of course, but I thought you'd find it interesting."

Ouédrago.

After another series of hang-ups, there was Brad. "Glen. I think I saw you the other day in the East Village, but it took me a minute to realize it was you since I thought you were supposed to be back in Chicago. Then Salif mentioned bumping into you, so I figured it must have been you. Anyway, I thought I'd check how it was going and see if there was anything I can do."

So that had been him at the funeral the other day with Issa. But whose funeral could it have been? And what had they exchanged in that velvet pouch?

"Oh, and whenever you've got a moment, I have something to give you. It might be just what you've been looking for."

Another sign.

The next message was from Grace at the museum. In a crisp, authoritative tone, she said she wouldn't need me to report back as they were fully staffed with volunteers. A chill passed through me. Had she discovered my removal of the paper fragment from the museum?

"As your area of study lies outside the immediate concerns of the museum's agenda," she went on, "we feel that you'll be a better fit elsewhere." What the hell did that mean?

After that, there were a few more hang-ups, then silence. I deleted all the messages and pulled out the scrap of paper I'd discovered in the house earlier. It was curiously similar to the Visconti decks.

Upon closer inspection, I noticed a thin blue and gold border, just like the one on the original cards. What little was left of the image had been lightly chipped and faded away in that subtle yet definite way only centuries can manage.

I pulled out my own reproduction of the original deck. Spreading the cards over the kitchen table, I could find no card with a missing corner. However, four of the cards from the original deck had never been found, and two of them — the Devil and the Tower — were missing from the Major Arcana. There was a good deal of debate over whether or not those two cards had ever been included in the original deck or not. Modern reproductions designed for use in fortune telling had recreations of the cards based purely on speculation over how they might have looked if they actually existed.

What if this was an actual fragment of one of those missing cards?

Be patient.

My dealings with the people at the historic museum were not finished just yet, I decided. Maybe I could use Eileen as a way back in.

But before I could worry about sifting through an old house for scraps of painted paper, I had to focus on one of the most difficult tasks of my life. I called the airline and changed my flight to Chicago to tomorrow.

Chapter Nine

NINE OF SWORDS

Grief, loss, mourning. Misery, concern. Sadness. Miscarriage. Anxiety over a loved one. Suffering.

Eight slender silver objects cross over each other at right angles, each bearing a golden handle at one end, a sharpened point at the other. Through the center of the diamonds formed by their intersection, a ninth pointed object cleanly severs the entire confluence into two perfectly symmetrical halves.

October 25, 11 p.m.

I awoke from terrible dreams of the endless corridor. Hospital gurneys heaped with white mounds raced past me in all directions, the sound of their wheels against the floor getting louder and louder until they became the sound of hammering footsteps in the distance. And at the same time, the pounding seemed to be coming from beyond the doors I was running past, as if behind each one someone was trying to escape. Then suddenly, I was inside one of the rooms with Eileen taking my face in her hands. As her lips descended upon mine, I felt the shadow of someone coming up from behind me, and I knew that having allowed myself this distraction, it was too late to escape.

I woke in a violent sweat. I packed a bag quickly, determined to get to Chicago as fast as I could. As we whipped over Queens on the elevated subway track, Manhattan grew smaller and smaller, until it was little more than a tangled forest of industrial waste littering a narrow island at the edge of the ocean.

When I got to the airport, I discovered the flight was delayed by weather. Never had I felt so trapped. As the boards filled with delays and cancellations, I kept picturing my mother as I had last seen her: tiny and helpless. What if I didn't get there in time? Why had I gone away? I couldn't find a comfortable place to read or even a quiet place to think. I just paced the terminal.

When we finally boarded, the plane seemed to climb in slow motion, and the short journey seemed to take forever.

It is time.

Finally, I was standing at the door to my parents' condo. Dad answered the door, and Mom was standing right behind him, eager for a hug. When I pressed her to me, her head came up only to my chest, and her entire frame seemed to weigh no more than one of my arms. She eased herself down into her chair as Dad hugged me in turn. He patted me twice on the back, and in that gesture I heard, "It's going to be okay."

"I really wish there was something I could do, Mom. I feel so helpless."

"I know, honey. There's nothing anyone can do. Not even the doctors."

"You don't have to go through the chemo for me, you know. I mean, if you want to do it, I'll stand by you, but you don't have to do it because you think you owe it to me to fight this." It had taken everything I had inside me to let her know that she could simply rest if she had to, but then it came out like I was asking her to hurry up and die. "I mean, I love you, Mom, and I don't want to lose you, but I don't want to see you suffer even more."

"I know, Glen." A few tears rolled down her sunken cheeks, but she ignored them and pushed on. "I told your father that before I went into the hospital for the operation, I had just stocked the pantry, so you'll find those crackers that you like in the back near the other snacks."

"Mom, don't worry about it. I'll be fine."

"I tried to get the brand that you told me about last time, but I wasn't sure whether you liked the onion kind or the sesame, so I got the onion. I should have picked up both. I'm sorry."

It was sheer agony listening to her waste her energy fretting over these trivial details. She insisted on taking us through the house, showing us where she had tucked away her most precious belongings — her photo albums on the top shelf of the hallway closet, her mother's costume jewelry in the back of her bottom dresser drawer, and her grandmother's china in the back of the storage locker — in a tiny padlocked cage in the concrete block storage locker down the hall from their condo.

She tried to manage these objects as she had before the illness, attempting to lift each of them herself before we could offer to help. To tell her that we didn't want her to go through this effort for our benefit would have been to deny her whatever closure she felt it would provide for all of us, but to watch her struggling with these things in her condition was unbearable. Instead of sitting down to talk about how much she meant to us and how much we would miss her, we had to rescue her from the burden of all the cartons and cases she kept unearthing from storage.

My father and I played along as best we could, listening to her instructions and responding with assurances. "This china belonged to my grandmother, and the pieces will really be worth something. Once I'm gone, you can have them appraised and sell them."

"Mom, I don't want to sell them."

"No, I want you to. You never knew my grandmother, so these wouldn't mean anything anyway. I've been saving them for you because I knew this day would come, and now maybe I can leave you something that's valuable. Be sure you find out how much they're really worth before you sell them."

"Okay, Mom."

This ritual passing on of the family treasures, I began to understand, was something she needed to do. Given her proximity to death, her wishes took precedence over any opinions my father and I might have. We could not argue, for suddenly she was wiser than either of us.

Yes, just listen.

It was in the storage locker, behind the carton of her grandmother's china wrapped carefully in tissue paper, that we came across the old shoebox.

"Here it is!"

She knocked the lid to one side and rustled through the tissue paper that protected its contents, revealing a colorful scarf…the one that wrapped my great-grandfather's cards I'd played with as a child.

"Granddad would tell us stories with these," she said. She seemed to have forgotten she was sitting on the concrete floor of the storage room. Her eyes were glazed over with a thick cloud of memory.

"Come on, honey." My father started helping her up. "We'll go back inside."

"Take that with you, Glen. I want you to have them."

I picked up the shoebox and put the lid back on as Dad helped her up, placing her thin, brittle arm around his shoulder. But the movement was too much for her, and she let out a shriek.

I tried to imagine the cancer moving inside her. Was it a single evil entity that oozed through her body like a blob in a science fiction film, or was it a series of individual cells working together like an army? Did it have any sort of a personality? Or perhaps it was more like a poison that blocks the life-maintaining functions of the body.

How much of my mother's pain was caused by the cancer's destruction of her tissue, and how much was from the surgical scars? How greatly was the pain exaggerated by her cognizance of what was happening inside her?

Mom was exhausted from the trip down the hall. Back in the condo, she lowered herself to the sofa, as I placed the box on the coffee table.

"Open it," she said.

"You should rest," Dad said, but she wasn't having any of it.

"I want to see!" she barked.

So I pulled out the cards, still wrapped in the scarf. Also in the box were some old letters, coins, rings, a rusty pocket knife, some wooden rosary beads, and a tarnished sterling silver watch on a long chain with an intricate fob.

"Those were all my grandfather's," she said.

"What was he like?" I asked her.

She opened her mouth to answer, but then her face scrunched in confusion. "He… I… Oh, god, what were we talking about?"

No more questions. The answers will come.

We put her to bed with a bit of the morphine the doctors had prescribed for pain.

Once she was safely asleep, my father confided in me. "It's been so hard since she's been back from the hospital. She just keeps saying, 'When the time comes, pull the plug.' But then in the next breath, she says she wants to go through with the chemo. And then she flies off the handle at the littlest thing. I feel so helpless. As terrible as it is to say, I… Well, I wish it could just be over."

I put my arms around him, and he sobbed on my shoulder. It was an almost unbearably awkward moment. Not that I was uncomfortable with the physical gesture of hugging my father or expressing my concern for him. But the moment I touched him, I could feel him trembling from deep within. For that second, he felt as tiny and fragile as my mother. If he cracked up, what could I use to support him?

We made a couple of sandwiches and sat out on the balcony, talking as the sun set, looking out at the suburban geometry spread before us, rows and rows of identical houses bathed in deep oranges and reds.

Back inside, Dad poured us a couple of scotches while I sat on the couch. I picked up the cards and unwrapped them from the scarf Mom had always kept them in. Why had Mom been so secretive about this deck until now?

Peeling back the covering, I discovered that Mom had returned the cards to what was presumably their original packaging: a faux leather box with the Highlanders logo embossed on its tattered cover. A pair of one-cent proprietary tax stamps marked the surface, suggesting they must have been over 100 years old. Manufactured by

L.I. Cohen, N.Y., the box said. Amazing, even if this deck was little more than a standard one of the time.

I slid the cards out of the box. They were yellowed with age, and worn at the edges from frequent shuffling. True to the cards of the mid-19th century, there were no Roman numeral indices in the corners of the cards, just the images themselves, though the suit cards in this deck were marked with "K" for King, "Q" for Queen, etc.

Yet despite their simplicity, my great-grandfather had clearly thought these cards important enough to pass down to his heirs.

Dad handed me my drink and noticed me shuffling through the old deck. "So how do these babies rate in terms of their historic significance?" His genuine interest in my work reminded me of his great faith in me. Would I disappoint him?

"Well, they're clearly old," I said, trying to sound as authoritative as possible, "but they're really nothing but a standard pack of playing cards, so they're not of any use in my study of the Tarot. It is interesting, though, to see how the packaging of those earliest American decks is reminiscent of the more eclectic Tarot decks." I continued flipping through the cards as I spoke, landing on an image that was totally incongruous with the others in the pack.

The Hanged Man.

Or so I thought at first, but then I realized the card was smaller than the others. It was actually a holy card that had been inserted into the deck — probably for safe keeping — depicting the inverse crucifixion of Saint Andrew in a vaguely Greek Orthodox design. "'The patron saint of fishermen and unmarried women who hope to bear children,' it says here. Was Mom's grandfather a fisherman?"

"Well, no. I mean, I don't see how he could have been. They lived in the middle of the prairie ever since arriving in America."

"Why must people take their secrets with them to their grave? It makes understanding the past almost impossible."

"Yeah, but just think: If everyone left complete records of their life and work, historians would be out of a job."

"True." We had a chuckle over that one, but I was left unsettled by the presence of the holy card in the deck. Had it been placed there merely to keep it safe among the other cards? Or had it been used as a part of the game? And what had given these cards such meaning to my great-grandfather that he passed them down as a family treasure?

He wanted you to see.

"So how is your work going?" Dad asked, catching me off guard.

"Oh, it's going…" I continued flipping through great-granddad's cards, looking for words to explain my vision to my father. How could I tell him that I just knew I was onto something, though I had not a single shred of evidence? "I think I found an important missing link in the cards' history, but I don't want to jinx it."

And then it hit me like a sledgehammer. On the nine of spades, in the middle of the symbol at the very center of the card was a thin ocher smudge. And the moment I saw it, I knew exactly what had formed it, just as I knew what had created the smudge on the card I had seen at the Morgan library.

Blood.

Of course it could have been a thousand things, but wasn't that exactly the color of dried blood? Wasn't that its exact texture? There was no way to be sure without testing. And, anyway, maybe *The African Origins of the Tarot* had planted an idea in my head about…

Sacrificial blood.

This was not the time to probe further, not in front of my father. I put the cards back into their box and pretended not to notice anything.

I had to help Dad. That was my job right now. He said he was going to sleep in the guest room, leaving me the living room couch. "I've been sleeping alone ever since bringing her back from the hospital," he explained. "I tried sleeping with her, but it hurts her to be touched, and she needs the entire bed to toss and turn on. And now, I have to save my strength…"

"You're doing all you can."

He thanked me with a quiet sigh and went to bed.

I poured myself another nice shot of scotch from the decanter in the dining room, picked up great-granddad's cards and slipped them into the outer pocket of my suitcase. My hand brushed against the book inside. I pulled it out, surprised to see the French words on its cover. I hadn't remembered bringing the Ouédrago text with me.

Flipping through the pages, I lingered over the images of "totems" prevalent in Western Africa. Many looked like large forked tree trunks, notched with stairs and doubling as ladders when balanced against mud brick homes. Others looked more like statues — depicting animals or even people. There was a carving of a fruit bat, hanging upside down from a tree by one leg, the other leg crossed like that of the Hanged Man in the Tarot.

Never an accident.

The more I read about the role of totems in African society, the harder it was for me to grasp the concept behind them. I thought at first that "totem" referred merely to a sacred object used in ceremonial rites — a statue or mask depicting a divinity or a tool such as a ladder used to reach the divine. However, it seemed that my very literal, modern sensibility was clouding my ability to grasp the broader range of the animist beliefs. A totem could also be a sacrificial animal. The sacrifice was a celebration, and the sacrificed animal as a totem was actually a god. By eating of its body and blood, the living ingested the deity. A powerful enemy could also be sacrificed as a totem.

The Naarem, on the other hand, was a tool of *divination*, which meant the reader was attempting to see with the eyes of the *divine* or *playing god*. But in a tradition in which god was in everything, it was possible that divination was not so much about playing god as *playing with god*. And if they were painted with actual blood, then how much more powerful was the essence of their spiritual center?

I poured myself another scotch. A double. What if the pigmentation in the cards contained not only blood but other animal and/or human residue? Blood, bone dust, semen, feces, brain matter.

Perhaps the original Naarem had evolved as Ouédrago said it had, through religious ceremonies of initiation in Western Africa. It might then have migrated to Italy through early sub-Saharan trade routes. An Italian nobleman wishing immortality might have tried duplicating the ceremonial recipe, giving it a European flair with images from his world. Perhaps his illustrators used actual blood in the creation of their pigments to keep the cards authentic. Surely human sacrifice was not absent from the Middle Ages, when blood flowed like tap water in dungeons across Europe.

I'd hardly want to mention my speculative theories when asking to have the pigments of the card back in the library — one of the most treasured hand-painted Tarot cards in the world — examined for their properties. If it ever turned up, that is. Who had taken it? And why had it come to New York in the first place?

While dreaming up a more plausible argument for a professional analysis of the Visconti-Sforza deck, though, I could certainly have my granddad's cards tested. And if there were any sort of organic material on them, it would be important to find out how it got there. If it did turn out to be blood, maybe it would turn out to be his blood. Just as people once spit into their palms for good luck before rolling dice, card readers might have pricked their fingers before shuffling divinatory decks to physically infuse their spirits into them, a ritual habit that could easily have evolved from more elaborate forms of sacrifice as the ancient cards migrated across the world and through the centuries.

I found my heart pounding. Maybe I was going too far, too fast.

Just let the voice speak. Listen.

But what if those occultists who said the wisdom contained in the cards couldn't be explained in academic language were right? If the Tarot were actually capable of reaching into another dimension of reality via its symbolism, perhaps its language couldn't be transcribed in written language.

Follow the voice.

I took out my grandfather's cards and began shuffling them, concentrating on a question. I had no key to read the symbols on these "ordinary" suit cards, I realized with great impatience. I was used to the interpretive guides included in modern, published decks to flesh out my intuition with specific symbolic language. To read these cards, I needed to open myself to the possibility that they actually offered something more, something beyond their facades.

Listen.

I pulled one of the cards from the deck at random. It was the Jack of Clubs — the equivalent of the Page of Staves in the old Italian deck. That was the card I'd always selected to portray myself when conducting a reading.

I noticed what I assumed were my great-grandfather's fingerprints in the reddish-brown smudge on the card's surface. A wave of warmth passed through me. It was as if he'd been there for a second, and I suddenly knew that everything was going to be okay.

Soon she'll be here.

October 26, 5 p.m.

I asked Dad if I could spend some time alone with Mom today. I drove her out to Oakbrook shopping mall where we found a bench in the sunlight and watched people strolling around the carefully manicured gardens between stores. For the first time since she'd learned she had cancer, she glowed ever so slightly with the energy that made her Mom. She fixated on the shoppers darting in and out of Marshall Fields and Lord & Taylor, fascinated by their every move and feature.

"Do things seem different to you?" I asked.

"Not really. It's just that I know this is the last time I'll see them."

We didn't speak much. Occasionally, one of us would recall a moment from my childhood and share it. Mostly, we just sat quietly together. Mom had always been a woman of few words.

I had planned to ask her about her grandfather's cards, but suddenly I didn't have a question. I felt an incredible sense of gratitude. We were sharing this moment during which we were both alive and conscious and at perfect peace with one another.

You know the answer.

But then as if sensing my thoughts, she brought it up herself. "I always worried about your interest in that Tarot stuff, you know, because I knew what it did to my grandfather. He went completely crazy and ended up killing himself."

My mouth dropped open in shock. This was the first time I'd heard anything about his death. In fact, she'd never talked about her grandfather at all until now.

"That's what my mother always told us. She said he'd learned to read the cards from the son of an escaped slave who'd come to the Midwest on the Underground Railroad just before abolition. She called the cards 'black magic voodoo', and I guess I never thought to question her. But now I realize that a lot of what we thought back then was probably just prejudiced. That's how things were at the time."

I was stunned. I wanted to ask about the cards, about her grandfather, about so many things, but still I couldn't formulate any questions.

Just listen.

And then a question did come. "Do you still worry about me?"

"I used to think your soul was in danger, but now I can see that you'll be all right." She turned to look at me and her eyes welled with tears of pride. "You're a lot like my grandfather. He was a free spirit and so are you. Maybe in today's crazy world you've got a better chance than he had." She raised her frail hand to touch my face. "Go back to New York. I need to be alone with your father when it's time for me to go."

"But, Mom, you're not going to…"

"I don't want you hovering over me. It won't help."

She was growing tired, so I guided her to the parking lot and helped her into the car. "Amazing how fast it's all gone," she said, staring out the window. She didn't say another word the rest of the way home. She had drifted back into that place she'd been in ever since the cancer had been diagnosed — a place far from the living yet not quite among the dead.

As I drove back to the condo, a beam of sunlight broke through the clouds in the distance and reached down to the earth with a definitive stroke of brilliant, warm energy.

And that's how I knew that while my mother didn't need me right now to fight this, she would pull through, and despite everything the doctors said, she would be grounded again in this world.

Let it be.

Chapter Ten

THE DEVIL

Subordination, bondage, malevolence. Failure. Self-abasement, temptation, weakness of character. Black magic.

A giant horned man with the legs of a goat and the wings of a bat stands on a pedestal to which two smaller, subordinate creatures — one male and one female — have been harnessed. Bogged down in demonic clichés, the artist's rendering — designed to fill a gap in history — is hardly a visionary work of art. The image merely mimics another that may never have existed. Ironically, the very incongruity of the false illustration enhances its divinatory meaning, as if its sloppy symbolism were the very product of the weak will it represents.

When I came out of the dream, yesterday, I found myself wide awake, still falling through the air. My plane was landing in New York.

The moment I was on the ground, I felt a sudden urgent need to see Dr. Carter. But when I got to his office and told the department secretary that I'd come to see him, she said he was out until further notice with a medical emergency.

"What happened?"

"We don't have all the details, but it seems he's had a heart attack."

"My god. When…"

"It's been a few days now. He was very excited about something he'd just discovered at the Morgan library…"

"That was what I'd come to see him about."

"Oh, yes, you're writing on the Tarot, aren't you?"

"Yes."

"He told me to give you this."

She handed me a folded piece of paper.

"Is there any word on his condition? Can he have visitors?"

"He's stable, but for now they're restricting visits to only immediate family."

I thanked her and went into the hallway to unfold the piece of paper.

"Glen, Forgive me for having underestimated the importance of your work. Dr. Carter."

There was nothing more. Had it been his trip to the Morgan Library that had caused him to write this? Besides the disappearance of the card, what had he learned, and could it have actually caused him to have a heart attack? I was desperate to know, but it looked like there'd be no information till he was better. And not knowing the name of his contact at the library, I could hardly make the call myself.

Be patient and the answers will come.

As I unzipped the pocket on my backpack to tuck Carter's note away, I caught a glimpse of the old scarf containing my great-grandfather's cards, right where I'd slipped them before leaving Chicago. Where could I take these to have them tested? Brad said he knew a place I could take something. He'd said it would cost me, but this was definitely worth investing in. I wandered the halls hoping to bump into him, my mind racing. What if the questions I was asking weren't meant to be answered?

Just listen.

After touring the halls and finding no sign of Brad, I dug through the backpack in search of my calendar where I had his number jotted somewhere, but I must have left it at home. I could always stop by the restaurant...

And then I thought of seeing Brad at the funeral with Issa. Of course, I'd forgotten about the message he'd left on my machine. Something about him having something for me.

Breathe or you won't hear.

I needed a moment to pull my thoughts together, so on my way downtown, I ducked into the Empire State Building and purchased a pair of plain black dress socks from the old man, who barely lifted his eyes from the ledger he was writing in.

From the windows of his showroom, downtown looked like so many well-worn toy blocks, stacked like stairs up to the base of the Twin Towers. Beyond it all, the wide sweep of the harbor and the infinite complexity of clouds provided the perfect accent to the skyline, as if the neat, solid rows of buildings had come before the nature they were built from and the sky above existed only for aesthetic balance. And yet this skyline, however permanent and unbreakable it seemed, was entirely non-existent when the original images on the Tarot had been painted over 500 years ago.

Before heading back down into the streets and subways of the city, I ducked into the bathroom — one of hundreds of identical rooms in the building, each of them pulling tons of gallons of waters through the arterial plumbing system that has served as lifeblood to the structure for about three quarters of a century.

I had just locked myself in the wooden stall closest to the bulky old porcelain sinks at the entrance when I heard someone enter. Two pairs of dark brown dress shoes shuffled past the cubicles. Neither man said a word as they advanced deliberately toward the stalls at the very back of the room. One of them hummed a tune that was strangely familiar, though I couldn't quite put my finger on it.

I heard the creaking hinges of a stall door. The humming stopped mid-measure as the door creaked closed, then the humming resumed and the footsteps made their way back towards me.

The men took turns humming bits of the melody, which I now recognized as the *Morte o Merce* — music about the cycle of death from the 15th-century Aragonese Court of Naples. Not exactly the latest pop song. I could hear them opening each stall one at a time. The shoes stopped directly in front of my door, and I could hear a whispered exchange…in what sounded like Mooré, the language Issa and Salif spoke. In fact, it sounded like it could easily have been the brothers from the restaurant.

I found myself holding my breath, terrified, as if I had a reason to hide from them. The footsteps separated, and I could see one pair of shoes heading towards the sinks near the entrance, the other to the stall on my other side. The man at the sink turned on the faucets full force and continued humming, while the man in the stall locked his door decisively, never missing a beat in his musical collaboration with the other man.

But then the man in the stall beside me began speaking in English. "Midway upon the journey of our life," he said in time with the droning hum of his accomplice at the sink, "I found myself within a forest dark, for the straightforward pathway had been lost." His thick African accent was unmistakable. I was frozen helplessly to the spot. What did they want?

The sound of a flushing toilet was followed by the stall door banging open. The man joined his friend at the sinks. He washed his hands as they chatted in what sounded like Mooré but could have been any one of a hundred African languages, as far as my untrained ears could tell. And then they were gone.

As I exited the bathroom, the elevator doors were already closing, so I never got a look at the two men to know whether or not they were Issa and Salif or just two random guys. I was creeped out the whole way home, paranoid I was being followed.

No accidents.

The English words he'd chanted haunted me. They were strangely familiar, somehow, though I was fairly certain they weren't from the *Morte o Merce*, which had a Petrarchan sonnet for its lyrics, if I remembered correctly. No, these words were like something from a dream that can't be shaken even long after waking from it. I jotted the words down as closely as I could remember them and went straight home to look them up.

9:40 p.m.

"*Nel mezzo del cammin di nostra vita mi ritrovai per una selva oscura ché la diritta via era smarrita.*" The first line of Dante's *Inferno*.

I couldn't come up with a logical reason why the brothers would have followed me. But despite any concrete lack of evidence, I *felt* it had been them and that they had followed me there deliberately.

I called Brad to see if he could shed any light on things.

"Glen! Good to hear from you. I wanted to tell you, I've got this book for you on secular art during the Renaissance. It doesn't mention the Tarot, but you still might find it useful."

"Thanks for thinking of me. Hey, did you hear about Dr. Carter?"

"Yeah, it seems like it was a case of stress. They're saying it's minor but he had a real scare."

"Well that's good news, I guess... I saw Issa and Salif from the restaurant today." It slipped out of me suddenly and awkwardly, with the force of an accusation.

"Uh, I don't think that's possible, my friend, because they had to leave town in a hurry."

"Really, what happened?"

"The restaurant got inspected after you left, and the Ouédrago brothers got deported. I heard they went to Montreal."

Ouédrago.

"That's their name?"

"What name?"

"You said Ouédrago."

"Oh yeah, I think it's something like that."

"So they didn't have working papers?"

"What do you think?"

"I guess I thought their family was here. I mean I saw you and Issa at that funeral. It must have been someone close."

"You mean the funeral parlor in the East Village? Uh, that's actually best not talked about over the phone." He sounded miffed.

"It has to do with the Naarem, doesn't it?"

"The what?"

"The African Tarot. Look, I know that Issa and Salif are into magic."

Brad started laughing so hard I had to hold the phone away from my ear.

"Glen, they're not into selling that kind of magic."

"Are you talking about drugs?"

"As I said, it's best not to talk about these kind of rumors on the phone. But before you get all judgmental, keep in mind that it's next to impossible, you know, for people coming from a country as poor as Burkina Faso to stay here legally and make ends meet. And they always intended to go home as soon as they'd saved enough. Anyway, I've got about four books to get through here. But try to lighten up, will you?"

I had meant to ask him about finding a place to test my great-grandfather's cards, but on second thought, none of that seemed important anymore. It wasn't about the physical details of the cards anymore but about something deeper.

You are listening now.

There was no way that I had stumbled upon the Ouédrago text and the two brothers — relatives of the author? — by accident. Could they really be selling drugs, or was that just a cover for something more...

More what?

Sinister? Earth shattering? Important?

Whatever it was, I wanted to know about it, and the secret, I was convinced, was in Africa. I was meant to go there. Hadn't everything I'd read on Africa so far told me that it was a continent full of oral, not written traditions? Hadn't it been impossible for generations of historians to shed light on the Tarot through book research alone?

I started surfing for airfares to Burkina Faso and realized it was going to cost a fortune. What the hell was I thinking? I figured it would take forever just to get a visa, but then I discovered a visa service that could issue one in twenty-four hours.

Go. Where you've been awaited for so long.

I had lost my direction, and I needed to find it again.

I was in the middle of planning everything I would need if I were to actually go through with the trip, when Dad called. Each time I hear his voice on the phone, a chill sinks into my spine, starting in my neck and shooting down to my toes. No, this couldn't be the phone call...

It's not the right time.

He said Mom was sleeping round the clock for the most part now. It was good that I had come when I did because she truly wasn't herself any more. The doctors were saying that she only had a month at most.

"Dad, we can't know that," I told him. "Her life force is strong. And when she wakes up and wants to see me, I'll be there."

I wanted to tell him that I knew she couldn't die just yet because I was being called on a long journey. But then I decided it would be best to keep all that from him right now. He wasn't ready yet, but when the time came, I knew he would understand.

Chapter Eleven

QUEEN OF SWORDS

A sharp, quick-witted person who is intensely perceptive. One who knew great happiness but who now knows the sorrow of misfortune. Fleeting pleasure.

She sits proud and tall, her long, white gown flowing from her, surrounding her throne. The golden crown she wears blends into the gilded background, and her elbow-length armored gloves match the silver of the sword she holds in her right hand. Her left is raised as if to stop an opponent or to bless an ally. Her face is as white as a mask, with the visible eye as black as a punched-out hole. At first glance, she seems to be smiling, but her parted lips could merely be poised in preparation for a verbal attack. Though she is supremely confident, there is a permanent rigidity in her stance. She is destined to eternally defend her throne.

I woke just now from the corridor nightmare. The tower, I realize now, is a great steel and glass one of hundreds of floors. Never have I seen the man who pursues me, though he is forever calling out a menacing chant in a language I can't understand. It has the rhythm of an African tongue, but I know with the knowledge that infuses my dreams that it is the language of some mysterious fraternal order responsible for introducing Naarem as the Tarot into the Western World. My dream wisdom also lets me know that the man is pursuing me because he suspects me of possessing incriminating evidence about his sect, but as I am unable to remember what documentation I've uncovered or where I've placed it, I can't begin to negotiate and must flee his wrath.

As I run away, I turn to catch a glimpse of him, but he is always just beyond the last corner or curve. All I can see is his shadow cast on the floor and the fluttering edge of his white embroidered robe. Finally, I come to the door of Steinbacher's Sock Shop. It's locked. I pound frantically, and the door opens. On the other side is Botu Mosabwe, the psychic from Tottenville, who is also Eileen from the museum in the East Village. In fact, the woman is constantly morphing between dozens of personalities and appearances, just as the room she invites me into continuously shifts from the interior of Botu's home at the edge of Staten Island to the parlor of the historic East Village home to a bookstore in the West Village to the office of Dr. Carter…along with so many other locations. In the strange logic of the dream, these faces and places are synonymous.

Once I'm inside, she slams the door behind me and double-bolts it, as if conscious of the threat awaiting me in the corridor. On a crudely carved wooden table inside the door, a large pile of gilded Tarot cards are arranged in two piles. With a silent wave of her hand, she invites me to reassemble the piles into one. As I do so, I discover I'm shaking. She pulls the top card from the deck just as an ominous pounding on the door shakes through the room. I suddenly realize we are in a vast and ancient library, the towering walls lined with shelves of dusty books as far as the eye can see. At tables set back into the shadows, bloody scraps of flesh (the remains of recent sacrifices) are crawling with flesh-eating beetles. The sight doesn't panic me, somehow. Instead, it serves as a confirmation of the inevitability of the visit, which I understand will crystallize the meaning of my very existence once and for all.

Holding up the card she has drawn, she squints disapprovingly at me — her icy stare blaming me for the image. It shows the collapse of a great earthen structure — more like a tree than a tower — that has been entangled with roots and vines as well as corridors and staircases. Though the card never moves on its own, I am aware of its infusion with a powerful life force. Suddenly, I realize that the structure it depicts is precisely the one we're standing within. A wave of terror passes through me like an electric shock. The pounding at the door increases to a deafening level and cracks across the building's floors begin to spread. As I fall through a crack, I realize the entire structure is being vaporized into a thin, chalky dust.

I awoke in a cold sweat. The dream was far more intense than usual. There was an urgency to it that stayed with me long after I was up. The images were at once vividly immediate yet completely unfamiliar. Something about the texture of the surfaces and the sounds made them crisper and more realistic than anything I'd dreamed before, as if someone else had written the dream and staged it with the help of a film crew. Upon waking from the crumbling tower, in fact, I had the distinct impression that the dream wasn't my own.

You're beginning to see.

The most lingering image was that of the strange tower card. Even after waking, I could sense the life contained within and emanating from that card. I thought of Aleister Crowley's claim that each of the archetypal cards was a living being.

A soul.

I felt compelled to conduct a reading, almost daring the tower card to turn up as it had in the dream.

But it didn't. Instead, I found the Queen of Swords in the first position, representing the present. My mother? Eileen? The crossing card was the Moon.

That card seems to be constantly looming over my readings like a threat. Who is the Moon? Another woman? Or is the feminine aspect of the card to be taken less literally, and could it be that the Moon represents something larger? Conflict was sprinkled throughout the reading in the form of many swords, and the presence of the Knight of Swords and the Chariot suggested travel. There was a trusted and stabilizing force in the past — the Page of Cups.

The reading was inconclusive, and as the light of day began to wash away the memory of my dream, I began to wonder if I hadn't exaggerated the intensity of the whole experience. But then I thought again of the strange tower card. What did it represent? The Tower was the only Major Arcana besides the Devil that remained absent from the original 15th-century deck, I reminded myself, and the attempts by contemporary artists to paint the "missing" cards to form a complete deck only made the notion that these cards may never have existed more compelling. The horned Devil card, for example, seemed like a ludicrous exaggeration of Christian mythology next to the other, subtler images in the deck.

Perhaps the inclusion of the tower in my dream was a message from my subconscious to examine missing links.

Explore. Listen. Trust.

I decided to take inventory and got out everything I had uncovered so far on my search for the origins of the Tarot, spreading the collection out on my desk: the notes I'd taken while viewing the original 15th-century cards, the text on the African origins of the Tarot, the painted scrap I found in the East Village museum, my great-grandfather's well-worn cards, dozens of books, and an imposing stack of other miscellaneous texts and references I'd acquired over the past several years.

But at that precise moment, it all seemed to me to be nothing more than a big pile of paper. Discouraged, I opened my great-grandfather's deck and began gently shuffling it. What had drawn him to these cards, and why had I become interested in them several generations later?

I fanned out the deck. Besides their slight discoloration, they were almost identical to contemporary playing cards. I rearranged them into one neat pile and placed them face down on my desk, where the fragment from the museum also happened to be lying face down. The pattern on the backs of both the fragment and my great-grandfather's cards were identical. Though the card from the museum was obviously far more tattered, it bore the same interlacing loops, which looked almost like the cursive letters students were once required to copy in grade school.

And then suddenly I realized what the pattern spelled. Just like the back of the card found in the museum, the back of each of my great-grandfather's cards repeated — in a series of tiny interlocking curlicues — the word "Naarem."

When my eyes grew weary from squinting to study these astonishing details, they moved up the wall towards the window to look over the city, but first they settled on the image of the little white tourist in the card Salif had given to me more than a week ago. So much had happened since then.

So much more to come.

October 31, 2:30 a.m.

I spent the rest of the afternoon researching Burkina Faso on the Internet. It's a landlocked country about the size of Colorado, just north of the Ivory Coast and Ghana. Around ten million people live there — among them are more than sixty ethnic groups speaking about as many languages and hundreds of dialects. French is the lingua franca. Each year, as global warming advances, the Sahara Desert grows, claiming more miles of land to the south and eliminating more of the nation's water supply. As the country depends entirely upon agriculture for its survival, the future of the nation's economy is bleak at best. Somehow, though, Ouagadougou, the nation's capital, has established itself as the location of a biannual pan-African film festival called FESPACO. It's also the hotbed of just about every one of the world's worst diseases, from the deadliest strains of malaria to cholera and guinea worm (a parasite that enters the foot and crawls up through the body).

Despite the bleak figures, most sources I consulted agreed that the population is among the friendliest in all of Africa. As the nation has barely been exposed to tourism, the traditional cultures of its many different ethnic groups have remained relatively unspoiled by globalization.

I called a vaccination service center in Manhattan. They could take me immediately. I dropped my passport at the travel document services office and ordered the visa for Burkina Faso, putting a rush on it. Then I crossed over to the vaccination place in the lower forties, where I was escorted into a small examination room filled with heavy metal furniture and fixtures left over from the 1950s. A few minutes later, a squat old man entered with my paperwork clipped to a board. "Burkina Faso," he said with little enthusiasm. "Cholera, malaria,…" He rattled off a few other diseases as he prepared the injections. "You'll need a booster for hepatitis in about six months." There was a whole list of follow-up steps — all of them written on the generic instruction sheet he handed me as I exited ten minutes later. The most important thing to remember was to take my mefloquine pill once a week to prevent getting malaria. I was supposed to start them a week before my trip. I popped my first one in the hallway, swallowing it with water from the rusty fountain near the men's bathroom before returning to the ground level on the creaky elevator.

Stepping out onto the street, I walked right into Eileen.

Never an accident.

"Glen!"

"Eileen. How random."

"Yes… Listen, I feel terrible about what happened at the museum. Grace can be fussy."

"I guess it wasn't meant to be."

"Well, I don't know about that. You had the perfect amount of interest and experience."

"Hey, want to get a coffee?"

We ducked into a little diner across the street and found a private booth near the back.

"What brought you up here?" she asked.

"Oh, just going to my six-figure job in Midtown."

"Really, that's exactly what I was doing! Actually, I live over in Hell's Kitchen."

"I was getting my travel vaccinations."

"Where are you going?"

"Well, I haven't bought my ticket yet, so I don't want to jinx it. I feel like I'm right at the edge of a great discovery, and all I need to do is take this one last journey."

"That's kind of where I'm at. Only for me, it's not about travel so much as just getting out of that old house. I feel like I'm at a point with my painting that I could break through to another level, if only I allow myself to find that next thing…whatever that is. God, I sound really flaky."

"Not at all. I'm all about listening to signs. They're there, you just have to be receptive to them. But I didn't know you painted."

"Yes. I haven't had anything shown yet, though. I mean outside of school."

"It will happen when it's time."

"That's what I think."

She blushed, and I leaned towards her. Our lips brushed. I pulled back and she was smiling. "I've been wanting to do that ever since I met you," she said.

"Me too."

"I hate people who make out in public, though. And now I'm guilty of doing it myself." She giggled. "I don't usually do this, Glen, but… God, that sounds like a line out of, I don't know… Okay, do you want to come back to my place? Jesus." She buried her face in her hands for a second, and when she looked up at me again, she was redder than ever.

"I'd love to."

"You're so serious," she said.

"I guess I am."

"I like that."

She lived in a railroad flat on the fifth floor. We walked up the narrow stairs, and she closed the door, pressing herself against me in a kiss before we could catch our breath. We pulled apart, gasping slightly for air, then kissed again, deeper.

As we made love, I found myself grounded again in my physical being for the first time in ages. The Moon was not my mother or Eileen, I realized, but Mother Earth calling me to engage with the physical reality of life again. I would go to Africa.

We made love frantically, as if all our creative energy had manifested itself physically at the place where our bodies connected.

You've always been welcome.

The next thing I knew, I was waking from the dream about the collapsing tower. Only this time, in my explorations of the corridors, I came upon a room decorated like the set for some old Hollywood movie about an African cult full of voodoo stereotypes. A group of about twenty people dressed in tribal masks gathered around a young woman who'd been blindfolded and tied to a large round table wearing nothing but her underwear.

A tall thick man whose face was concealed entirely by a narrow wooden mask placed thorny long-stemmed roses on her body, gently positioning them between the lace of her lingerie and her delicate skin. She trembled in anticipation as he caressed her with the petals of each flower before gently slipping the thorny stems into position near her breasts, her inner thighs. The participants chanted in a strange language as they danced around the woman, accompanied by African drums.

Suddenly, each of the participants in the circle grabbed at the flowers, dragging the thorns against her body as they ripped them from her. The petals broke away from their stems with the violence of the motion, fluttering in all directions. The woman's scream — of pain mixed with pleasure — seemed to be coming from all directions at once, and I felt the foundation of the building shake. The collapse was painfully slow and deafening. The darkness of the billowing dust, which the crumbling structure had instantly become, was deeper than the blackest recesses of any sea.

I snapped awake in a cold sweat, feeling more disoriented than I have ever felt in my life. It took me a good five minutes to remember where I was...who I was. I had no recollection of having fallen asleep. Come to think of it, I couldn't even remember pulling apart from Eileen, though we were now on separate sides of the bed. My head hurt as if from a terrible hangover, though I'd had nothing to drink all day.

"What's the matter?"

"I'm fine. I had a nightmare."

"You poor thing."

I couldn't bear to have her touch me. "I should go home."

"You can stay here," she said, trying to caress me. But I was already standing, searching for my clothes among the garments we'd scattered on our way into the bedroom. I needed my own space.

"I really should go."

"It would be nice if you stayed, but if you don't want to..."

"I just can't right now. I'll call you."

Soon, I was on a subway car headed for the ferry in the middle of the night. By the time I was on the boat crossing the harbor, Eileen seemed no more tangible than the tower in my dream. My head ached, and there was a mood of utter dread left over from the dream, though as its images grew fainter, I could no longer find a single tangible impression of it. I knew only that I was about to experience something of monumental importance.

3:15 a.m.

At home, there was a message from my father saying he just wanted to talk — nothing new. A slight tremble in his voice betrayed his fear and sadness. For a second, I considered booking a ticket back to Chicago, but then I knew that was not what was meant to happen right now. No longer could there be any distractions from my destiny.

Chapter Twelve

KNIGHT OF STAVES

Departure, flight, absence. Change of residence. A journey into the unknown.

The boy with the blond curls rides an armored steed. The snow-white creature kicks up its front legs, twisting its mouth against the bit in a violent whinny. Though the boy has aged since his last appearance as a page, he retains his fragility, but his eyes have grown wide and dark. Dwarfed by the massive beast, the boy's lips are, nevertheless, pursed with the confidence of a fearless soldier charging into war. He hasn't noticed that his horse's eyes have rolled back, as if the creature were trying to see his rider to warn him about the great danger they are about to embark upon. The boy is conscious only of their swift movement forward.

The dream keeps getting more intense as it grows more familiar. I no longer wake up in a blur, trying to decide where I've been. Now I remain inside the tower while it crumbles, tumbling head over heels for dozens of floors. As I careen through the dust, bits of office supplies are scattered around me along with fluttering fragments of paper, some of them sacred texts. In that final moment of terror before waking, I am sure, somehow, of the rare importance of these lost documents, just as I'm sure that the woman with the roses is Eileen.

Sacrificed.

It was already 10 a.m. by the time the phone woke me. It was the travel document services center in Midtown. My visa was ready for pickup.

I was going to Africa. The idea washed over me with crystal clarity. There was no longer a question, not even a "Why?" It simply was.

Self-sacrificed.

I went online to try to purchase a ticket, but for Burkina Faso, tickets had to be shipped through snail mail, and there were no online student rates. I'd do better with an actual agent in town. So after picking up my passport and visa, I found a storefront agency specializing in student deals near Times Square.

"Fifteen," the agent called out.

I handed him the rectangle of plastic with the corresponding number. "I want to go to Burkina Faso as soon as possible… tomorrow, if I can."

He looked stupefied.

"It's in West Africa," I offered.

"Well, I know. I was just surprised because we don't get a lot of requests for it."

"The capital is Ouagadougou."

"Yes, I think the code is OUA…" He typed the letters into the computer. "Yeah, there it is." He studied my face again. "It's going to be a pricey one. At least two thousand if not more."

"Is there any way to bring it down with student discounts or anything?"

"Hard to go last minute to that part of the world without spending a lot of money, unless maybe if you go as a courier. You realize you need a visa, right?"

"Got it."

"And you should have your vaccinations up to date as well as something to prevent malaria…"

"All taken care of. Do you offer courier fares here?"

"No, but I can put you in touch with a company that does. Though there may be a wait list…"

"Isn't there another way?"

"We can always get you a cheap student fare to Paris, then you can see if a consolidator based in Paris is able to sell you something on site…"

"If it will make the rates more affordable."

"If you're certain about making this trip, I could try to find a Paris-based consolidator who can deliver a ticket to you at the Paris airport."

"I'm definitely sure."

"It will still wind up being around a thousand."

"Fine."

I would fly to Paris on Air France, then someone would meet me in Paris at the Air Afrique gate with my ticket to Ouagadougou, exactly two hours before the Africa-bound flight departed. It was more than a thousand dollars cheaper than any other option. Plus it left me open to return whenever I wanted.

Just go.

"I'd be sure and reconfirm your Paris flight twenty-four hours before departure. Where will you be staying?"

I hadn't even considered where I'd be sleeping. That little oversight startled me, and I wondered for a second if this wasn't completely crazy of me after all. "Can you book something for me?" I asked.

"Well, usually only luxury properties show up in our reservation system, but let's see what we've got… Hmm, looks like there's not a single property in the entire country that's linked in. But I really don't think you'll have much trouble finding affordable accommodation on site in Ouagadougou. Of course, you can always check out the travel books over there." He nodded towards a rotating rack of *Lonely Planet*s and *Rough Guide*s near the door. I grabbed the first one I found with the words "West Africa" on the front and asked him to add it to my bill.

After charging everything to my card, he pushed the guidebook and ticket across the desk and into my hands. "Hey, be careful over there," he said.

"Thanks." I avoided meeting his eyes as I gathered my documents. He sounded more than a little worried, and I didn't need that kind of negative energy bringing me down, filling my mind with fear. This was meant to be.

Just keep listening.

Outside, I skimmed the travel essentials section in the guide right there in the street. Yes, I had all my vaccinations, but there were a few other things I still needed. I ducked into a Duane Reade to get mosquito spray, sunscreen and anti-diarrhea tablets, then I bought a portable water filter and purification tablets at a sports and camping store on Eighth.

These little efforts at preparing myself were reassuring. Travel supplies had been designed and used by millions of people before me who'd all rounded the globe in search of adventure. I was only flying to another country, not dropping off the face of the earth. Everything would be fine.

Confining my perusal of the guidebook to the logistical sections, I avoided all the passages on history and culture. My perspective at the moment was virtually untainted by preconceptions, and I wanted to maintain that.

I want to be completely open to every experience that comes my way over there. I'm heading to Burkina Faso with only the faint promise of the existence of something called the Naarem and a bit of intuition.

The beauty of it is that I can't be led astray by existing studies. There's only the one — incomplete and vague as Ouédrago's text is. I'm in a unique position, one that is at once terrifying and exhilarating. If I uncover any new information, I'll be looking at it with fresh eyes, unclouded by the constructs of previous researchers.

Open yourself to the voices.

I decided to cross over to the East Village on the chance Eileen might be working at the museum. I owed her an explanation of some kind for my abrupt departure the night before. It was all because of where I'm at with the journey I'm going on.

The house was well lit as I approached, though it was already past its opening hours. I rapped twice and heard footsteps approaching. Grace answered the door, her affected smile sinking into a frown as she recognized me. "Good evening. I take it you've come to ask me to reconsider my decision."

"Actually, I was looking for Eileen."

"Eileen no longer works here," she said bitingly.

"Oh."

"She…" Grace's explanation was arrested by the approach of someone from behind her. As she came into focus, I recognized her as Botu Mosabwe, the psychic from Tottenville.

She looked directly at me with a fixed and penetrating stare but offered no greeting. "Thank you," she said, turning to Grace. "I'm sure the event will prove to be an enormous success."

"Yes. I'm sure of it too."

"A renewed interest in the occult has led many people to seek answers in the time-honored traditions we've been led away from by our modern skepticism," the psychic said. Though she spoke to Grace, her eyes had come back to settle on me as she delivered her speech.

"Well, there certainly is a popular appeal to such activities."

"Are you going to be offering some sort of readings at the house?" I asked.

"It's a fund-raising event," Grace snapped. "Now, if you'll both excuse me."

Soon I was descending the front steps with Botu as the locks clicked shut behind us.

"She is full of fear," said Botu.

"Is that what it is?" I asked, looking up at her as we reached the sidewalk.

Botu's eyes welled with tears, suddenly, as she looked into mine. "And you have none, my child. None at all."

"I…"

"You must be careful on your journey. Very careful."

"Journey?" I asked, assuming she was speaking figuratively.

"Let the light find you," she said.

Listen.

"So what are you going to do for Grace?" I said, more to break the silence than out of any genuine interest.

"They're going to have a fund-raiser at $100 a person that includes dinner and admission to a midnight séance."

"Really! Interesting, because I got the idea she didn't want me as a docent because of my interest in the Tarot. She seemed to think I was biased."

"You are."

"What do you mean?"

"This séance is nothing but a costume ball for a bunch of bored old wealthy Manhattanites."

"So why are you…"

"To fund my real work."

"But how did Grace come up with the idea?"

"Eileen."

"Oh, you know each other?"

"Of course. Isn't that how you came into contact with me?"

"No, I found your flyer."

She laughed. "Oh, right."

No accidents.

"But what happened to her?"

"Who?"

"Eileen. I just saw her and she didn't say anything about…"

"Grace fired her because she knows more about the house than Grace does, and she let her know it."

Before I could formulate another question, she said, "It's Halloween — a night of disguises worn to ward off evil spirits."

We were crossing over Broadway now, and costumed revelers were everywhere. It was the usual assortment — witches, vampires, Marie Antoinettes, King Arthurs, serial killers, characters from popular films and current events — each created with a different degree of care and humor that revealed as much about the reveler's budget as his or her commitment to the annual ceremony.

A particularly convincing Death waved a scythe over our heads. In another context, the image might have spooked me, but here, in this cauldron of rubber masks and blinking devil horns it seemed somehow reassuring. We'd been blessed by the most immortal figure of them all.

Yes, listen.

"Here come the Sweepers," said Botu as we approached Sixth Avenue just in time to catch the beginning of the parade as it descended upon Manhattan.

"What are sweepers?" I asked.

"They're the giant puppets that lead the parade, sweeping all the negative energy out of the streets."

Each of the pallid papier-mâché figures was about three times the size of an average human and drifted above the crowd against the black sky, charging towards the spectators with arms fanned wide, as if preparing to scoop them up and eat them. Shrieking with delight, the crowd comforted itself with the knowledge these skeletal creatures were carefully controlled by the many puppeteers who operated them from below by holding the ends of the long, narrow sticks that supported them. Still, no matter how many times you saw the figures, it was hard not to shudder when a giant skeleton came rushing at you with its foot-long bony fingers going straight for your face as if you were about to be pulled up forever into the night sky.

"Do you know when the puppets first became a part of the Halloween tradition in New York?" I asked Botu. When I turned for her answer, she was gone. Either the crowd had swallowed us in different directions, or she'd deliberately abandoned me. I'd wanted to ask her so many questions. But now I was alone among the revelers. Somehow, I felt safe among them, yet apart. I watched the movement of the crowd as if it were being played out in slow motion. All the laughter and shouting seemed muffled, all the lights diffused.

And then something was thrust into my hand. Dressed as a circus clown, a guy was handing out what I took to be passes for a popular nightclub. I watched him cross the street then disappear into the crowd a bit further down.

Only after he disappeared did I glance down at his calling card. It was a reproduction of the Hanged Man from the original Italian deck. I looked at the spot in the crowd where the clown had disappeared, but he never re-emerged. I pushed through tight clusters of people to cross the parade route, then worked my way back into the crowd on the other side of the street.

Chapter Thirteen

THE CHARIOT

Trouble, adversity, turmoil. Conflicting influence. Travel. Urgent need to gain control of one's emotions. Rushing to a decision.

All but effaced by the weight of her thick golden cloak, the diminutive figure seated upon a towering wheeled platform holds a globe and scepter. Two wingèd white steeds pull her carriage forward with a steady, measured gait, never jostling her from her determined, unflinching stance. They squint back at her, chomping at their bits in anticipation of their release. A complex swirling pattern on the woman's garment is similar to the one repeated on the Hierophant's robe, but her fabric is solid gold. It disappears completely into the gilded background along with the objects she carries. The only detail that stands out against the image's golden shimmer is the woman's small, pale face, which floats above the scene like a waning moon. Given her ghostly presence, her identity and rank seem entirely tangential. Whatever royal powers her regal accessories once commanded have surely evaporated before her very eyes. The journey has become the entire purpose of her existence.

November 3, morning

As I checked in for my flight to Paris, the ever-changing dream of the collapsing tower continued to haunt me. In the most recent version, the corridors I passed through took on the look of a set from an old Vincent Price film. Under the Technicolor facade — dressed with velvet, fog, and crystal balls — I *knew* that actual blood had been shed somewhere. My cards were being read by one of the hooded figures who'd bound the young woman with the roses. He spoke few words, but his furrowing brow suggested he saw terrible things in the images he drew. As I struggled to catch a glimpse of the cards, I saw that they were blurry — not from my lack of focus, but from their constantly metamorphosing faces. Each one was animated like a frantic music video. And while my eyes struggled to fix on the images, the entire pack disintegrated into dust, followed by the table, the walls, and the entire tower. The deafening roar of the collapsing structure drowned out the critical last words of the reader, and I bolted awake, conscious that I had once again missed the dream's critical insights.

November 4 — on the flight to Ouagadougou

I took a sleeping pill on the flight to Paris and dozed for a few hours, but the wait at Charles de Gaulle was almost unbearable. Despite the fact that it was a major gateway to the busiest tourist city in the world, the airport was oddly deserted, and were it not for the French blaring from the overhead speakers, I'd have thought myself in the wrong country. Moving sidewalks and escalators made their strictly calculated trajectories — their looping black ribbons barely touched by human feet. Fluorescent bulbs in airport cafés buzzed, illuminating coolers fully stocked with Orangina and Perrier. Could it be a continuation of my dream, I wondered?

After waiting more than an hour, I bought a card for the payphone and called the company that was supposed to have sent a rep to meet me with my ticket to Africa, but an answering machine picked up. I went up to the Air Afrique agents and explained my dilemma. Just as I suspected, they had nothing to do with outside vendors. I waited at a bench near the ticketing counter with my luggage. Perhaps I wasn't meant to go to Africa after all.

It was only twenty minutes before the flight to Ouagadougou began boarding, and I was hatching a new plan. First, I'd change money into French francs, then go into Paris to find the office of the consolidator who'd sold me the ticket. I could stay in Paris and do some research on the increase in the popularity of the tarot in the 19th century as a divinatory tool. I would look up the Paris chapter of the Hermetic Order of the Golden Dawn that still used ancient Egyptian ritual...

I was lost in these thoughts when a tall African man in an intricately embroidered shirt approached me out of breath: "Excusez-moi. Monsieur...uh... Glen... uh..."

"Oui!"

The parallel tribal markings on his cheeks were thick and long. His giant bloodshot eyes never left the ground to meet mine. "I am sorry for to make you wait. I have problem with the *grève de métro*. All the workers of Paris have made a protest."

So there had been a citywide strike. Ah. That explained why the airport was so deserted. The man's accent reminded me of Issa and Salif's, but his voice was softer, and despite his tardiness, his manner was unhurried. "Sir, your flight from New York, it was good?"

"Yes. Thank you."

"And your preparations for the voyage were successful?"

"Um, yes." I was anxious to get on with our business and get on my way, but I had the feeling he'd gladly sit down to discuss my trip over a cup of espresso. He never once looked at me as he talked. Instead, his eyes seemed to study the tips of my shoes. Then I remembered reading in one of my guidebooks that it was considered impolite in African culture to stare someone directly in the eye, and his questions — which seemed almost prying to me — actually expressed nothing more than the minimum politesse required in a traditional African greeting. Usually, people didn't get down to business in Africa, it seemed, till they had asked about your health as well as the health of your immediate family, your distant cousins, your ancestors, and their ancestors. That my plane was boarding soon was of little concern compared with these formalities.

"Do you have a ticket for me?" I broke in.

"Oui, Monsieur." He pulled an envelope from inside his coat. If he'd perceived me as being abrupt, he made no sign of it. I suppose he was used to Westerners sidestepping formal greetings to get right down to business. "One ticket to Ouagadougou. You go to Burkina, huh?"

"Yes. I have to board the plane right away."

"Americans always in a hurry, eh?" Laughter shook his entire frame as if he'd just cracked the joke of the century. He finally caught his breath. "Oh, sir, Burkina will be very different pace, I think."

"I'm sure of it."

"But you will love Burkina. You will meet a Burkinabé woman and marry her, no?" He exploded into another trembling series of chuckles. "Our sisters are very beautiful."

"I'm sure. I'm actually going to work on my research."

"Yes, of course." He looked up to study my face for a moment as if to see if I were telling the truth. His eyes caught mine and held my gaze for a moment. I wasn't sure if he'd blessed or cursed me, but a chill washed down my spine.

You are almost home.

"Here is your ticket, and this is the case." He extended a well-worn leather suitcase to me.

I made no motion to take it. "What case?"

"Yes, someone will come to take it from you at the airport in Ouaga."

"But they didn't mention anything about a case."

He set it on the ground between us. "My friend, you have the special ticket because you have agree to transport the case." He pulled a wad of folded papers from the same pocket that had produced my ticket. It seemed he was about to go over every clause in the contract. I didn't have the time.

"What's in it?"

"That is not important for you."

"But I could get in trouble."

"You are not responsible for contents of case. And we are a professional company. I sign for case here, and you take it on plane with you, then a man in Ouaga he sign for to accept it when you arrive." Again, he caught my eye, and I felt another shiver pass down my spine. "I am not supposed to open it," he said. "But if you are more comfortable, who can know if I show you one time?" He pulled a large ring of keys from his pocket and searched for the matching one. "Not this one… no, not this one… Here he is!" Unlocking the briefcase, he flipped the latches and opened it right on the ground. Inside were papers, computer discs, and more papers.

I had no time to concern myself with the details. They'd just announced that my flight was pre-boarding, and I'd yet to check in and clear customs. "I'm sorry," I said. "It's just that I've never done this."

"Oh, there no reason for sorry, my friend." He shook with laughter as he pumped my hand with his in a friendly handshake. "Let us go check in bag, now."

At the Air Afrique counter, the man signed a form and was given a copy. Another was attached to the inside of my ticket folder along with my luggage tags. Apparently, this was an everyday occurrence. "Be sure and wait at the Ouaga airport for the person from the courier service to accept delivery of the case," said the agent mechanically. The man from the courier service pumped my hand again and wished me a safe and productive trip, then turned to the agent and waved. "*À plus tard*, Marie-France."

"*À ce soir*, Bokari," the agent called out after him as he departed.

So they'd known each other all along. They probably completed transactions like this several times each day. I felt reassured about the legitimacy of my ticket and the contents of the suitcase. At the same time I was unnerved at my own overreaction.

I'd have to loosen up if I was going to make a connection with the people of Burkina Faso.

Remember to always listen.

A few days (?) later

I've lost track of the exact date. Part of it is the jet lag, and part of it is that the actual calendar days and dates seem to matter less here. The only important divisions of time seem to be sunrise (when the world awakens), the middle of the day (when the heat is unbearable and everyone seeks shelter), sunset (when people prepare to sleep), and the black of night (when nothing stirs).

Flying over the Sahara was exhilarating. I had to keep the shade pulled down for most of the route because I could actually feel the heat through the window. Below, the flat sands stretched in all directions. Then, after several hours of this unforgiving landscape, tiny dots of green began to emerge on the landscape as it bled from gold into the reddish brown of the savannah. Soon, the plane was approaching the ground.

Approaching your destiny.

We stepped off the plane directly onto the tarmac, and the asphalt runway sizzled in the stifling heat. This was sub-Saharan Africa, all right. In the seconds it took to walk a few steps to the minuscule airport terminal, I was already dehydrated. I'm not sure why it surprised me, but I was immediately struck by the simplicity of the building — little more, really, than a squat concrete block with a broken luggage carousel and a couple of ticket counters. The smell of gasoline permeated the air. A stocky immigration officer with plump cheeks stamped my passport without ceremony and welcomed me to Burkina Faso. I'd been expecting more of a hassle, but this was easy.

Welcome.

After collecting my baggage and exiting to the arrival hall, which was barely larger than my modest apartment in Staten Island, I found a frail man with light brown skin and an angular face holding a sign with my name. He welcomed me to Burkina with a firm handshake then escorted me to a counter where he signed for the suitcase and an Air Afrique agent processed the paperwork with a definitive whack of her rubber stamp. The man directed me to the exit, where he said I would find a taxi, then disappeared into the confusion of exiting passengers who disappeared into vehicles, leaving thick clouds of red dust behind them.

A cluster of young men — some in their early twenties, some younger — clamored for my attention, trying to take my bags. "Taxi? *Monsieur, ici! Je vous donne le meilleur prix!*" They were dressed in worn t-shirts and frayed pants. Some had open sores attracting flies to their arms and legs. The afflicted men made only the slightest attempts to shoo the insects away — resigned, it seemed, to their presence.

I clutched my bags firmly, determined to follow the guidebook's advice in choosing a legitimate cab, but the very notion of "legitimate" seemed absurd as I glanced around at the tiny wrecks passing themselves off as transportation. Some had bumpers tied on with bits of rope, while others had frayed strips of clear packing tape instead of windows.

Of the dozen young men surrounding me, only one remained at a comfortable distance, while the others grabbed at my bags. The best-dressed of the group, he wore a sunny yellow V-neck shirt, which stood out sharply against his dark skin. He stood next to his vehicle, holding open the passenger door, inviting me inside with a silent sweep of his hand. *"Ma voiture est arrivée,"* I said to disperse the others as I moved to the young man's cab.

"Awwwww!" A collective moan went up from the crowd. The young men shoved at each other. *"Je l'ai vu d'abord!"* someone barked at my driver. He responded in a local dialect, generating a series of further objections. I had expected to be hounded by the drivers, not to be fought over. The group scattered, and soon I was being whisked away in the tiny cab on the bumpy roads of the West African city.

"Welcome in Burkina," the driver said to me in English. "My name is Idrissa."

"Merci. Je suis Glen. L'hôtel RAN, s'il vous plaît."

"You very serious man from America." The young man was beaming at me in the battered mirror that was cracked and taped together.

"I'm a very tired man from America."

"Long plane ride. It take many hours from Paris, then many more hours from America. It very beautiful in America, yes? Very rich."

"Not everyone is so rich in America," I said. But looking out the window now, I wasn't so sure that was true. Women carried massive plastic buckets full of grain and produce on their bare heads as they hiked on dusty, pothole-ridden roads where stray pigs, goats, and chickens ran free. Vultures oversaw the whole scene from telephone wires, waiting for one of the creatures below to become their next meal. It was too much for me after the long trip. I wanted to get to the hotel and shower before absorbing all this new information.

Breathe.

"I study English ten year now," he said proudly.

"You speak very well," I offered.

"What you come to Burkina to study?"

"The Tarot."

"What is Tarot?"

"It's…" I began to answer, when I realized I'd never mentioned I was in Burkina Faso to study anything at all. And I'd never mentioned I was from America. How had he known I wasn't from Europe or anywhere else for that matter before I'd even spoken enough words to reveal an accent? But perhaps he simply knew. That's why I had been drawn to him among the other drivers.

Listening now.

When I looked up, he was examining me in his rear-view mirror.

"It's a kind of game," I said. "Some call it the Naarem."

If he recognized the word, he didn't reveal the slightest indication of it.

"I think it originated here. In a place outside Gaoua."

"Gaoua is very far, but I know a man who can take you there."

"I was planning to take a bus."

"Yes, he take you to bus."

"Maybe tomorrow."

We had left the dusty roads of Ouagadougou's outskirts now and were rolling on the smooth pavement of the wide downtown streets. Vendors of African art lined the curb, packing every available inch of asphalt and concrete with every imaginable object: masks, statues, fabrics, electronics... Elsewhere, tiny makeshift restaurants fabricated out of sheets of corrugated iron hugged the curbs. And everywhere, mopeds — hundreds of them — zigzagged in and out of traffic, farting toxic clouds of petrol in their wake.

Suddenly, Idrissa turned right off the street. For a second, I thought we were going to drive straight through the vendors and their wares. I was sure we'd crush them, along with everyone else in our path, but then I realized we had actually exited onto a narrow driveway that slivered through the crowd. We were heading back into a cluster of palms that hid the RAN Hotel from the street.

One of the few buildings in the city that retained a French Colonial style, the RAN's arched windows and decorative, turret-like ornamentation maintained the image of an Africa few of the continent's residents had any reason to celebrate. A large awning extended to the horseshoe driveway as if awaiting the arrival of a horse-drawn carriage. Idrissa dropped me under it with a promise to return in the morning.

I was too exhausted to protest, and reached for my wallet to settle the fare but found it empty. "I haven't changed any money yet, so I can't pay you in francs. Let me go into the hotel and..."

He laughed. "No problem, my friend. I will come back tomorrow."

"But what if I..."

"Tomorrow."

"Okay." I stepped out of the cab, and a valet approached.

"Good afternoon, sir."

He greeted my driver. They shook hands, snapping their fingers together in the gesture Issa and Salif had taught me back at the restaurant in New York. Soon Idrissa's taxi squealed away, and I mounted the front stairs.

I couldn't believe I was finally in Africa.

Welcome home.

Later

After a couple of hours of sleep, I woke from a fuzzy dream to complete darkness and the nagging sense I'd made some sort of crazy mistake. Not that I was in any particular danger, but at the moment I was feeling that I'd run even farther from the answers I was searching for.

Strange, but this was the first time in ages that I'd woken up with no clear recollection of my dreams. It was as if a peaceful stillness had washed over my fears for a moment.

But then an intense sadness consumed me.

So far.

I pictured my mother sitting beside me in Oakbrook, watching the shoppers dart between the fading fall flowers.

You've already said goodbye.

I'm wiping away the last of my tears as I write this. Outside my window, a full moon is reflected in the pool below.

There's nothing I can do now but find the answers I've come for.

Chapter Fourteen

THE WHEEL OF FORTUNE

Destiny. Fortune. Culmination. Approaching the end of a problem. Unusual loss. Unexpected events. The inevitable course of things from beginning to end.

At the center of the massive spoked wheel, a blindfolded angel in a dark, flowing robe spreads her arms and wings. Embroidered with the same hexagonal solar pattern as the robes of the Hierophant and the Charioteer, her garment is silver on deep blue, setting her in stark relief against the golden background. Seated above her on a throne, a cherubic figure with the ears of an ass is dressed in a golden robe fading into the background along with the banner he waves. "Regno," it says. *"I reign."* To the angel's right, another dwarfish figure with the ears of an ass — this one dressed in bright green — looks up to the throne. "Regnabo," he whispers. *"I shall reign."* To the angel's left, another diminutive creature, this one dressed in red, clings frantically to the wheel to keep from falling. His face is pointed towards the ground, and his ass's tail wags in the air behind him. "Regnavi," he cries. *"I reigned."* Below them all, an old man crawls along the ground in rags. "Sum sine regno," he says. *"I am without reign."* Each one's time shall come.

November ?

On the plane home, delirious with fever, I try to write down some of what has happened. Have I been in Africa for one week? Two? My return ticket was originally scheduled for November 14, but I missed the flight. By how many days I'm not at all sure. When I arrived at the airport, they put me on the next available plane to Paris. I was so dizzy and sick — a parasite of some kind, I guess — I'm lucky they let me board at all.

Looking back at my journal, I see I left off with my arrival in Burkina Faso. That seems like years ago now.

I remember waking up the next morning with lots of energy, feeling like I was truly on the verge of something big. I stepped out the front door of the RAN to find Idrissa's cab waiting for me at the exact spot it had dropped me off the day before. Opening the passenger door, I startled my driver awake. Had he slept there, I wondered, waiting all night for me to emerge?

"Did Mr. Glen have good sleep?" he asked in a half-daze as his eyes came into focus.

"Wonderful," I said.

"Oh, that's very good."

Abruptly we slipped into the city's chaotic traffic, though I'd yet to announce where I was going. He tried insisting on taking me to his family's souvenir shop, but after five minutes of circling in the dense traffic while politely arguing about our destination, we finally pulled up to a corrugated metal shack by the side of a dirt road.

"I don't want to buy art, I just want to go to Gaoua."

"Yes, Bamako can take you to the bus."

A man emerged from the makeshift structure and approached my driver's window. They exchanged a long series of greetings in an African language (Mooré? Djula? Hausa?) as I waited. Though I'd learned the names of dozens of distinct languages spoken in the country, I couldn't tell one from the other, much less understand a word of any of them.

"Oh! You go to see the Lobi people, eh?" The man from the roadside shack was looking at me through the back window now. He couldn't have been any taller than five foot four, but his presence was as imposing as a giant's. His skin — the darkest I've ever seen — was crossed with thick parallel scars of an even darker hue. These raised slashes were repeated with perfect symmetry on each cheek. "Welcome," he said in rudimentary French. "That God protect you and grant you health on your journey."

"I'm going to Gaoua," I said.

"That is the town of my ancestors," he said. "Few tourists go there."

"I'm looking for information on the Naarem," I braved.

"Na...?"

"Naarem."

He betrayed no trace of recognition. "A village?"

"No, a sort of game or maybe a ritual. There was a book by Ouédrago. He was living with the Lobi."

He *tsked* and shook his head. "The journey to the Lobi is long and hard, my friend. Eight hours to Gaoua and then more to the villages."

"Is there a bus?"

He suggested a daily minivan, which took passengers west toward Bobo-Dioulasso along the nation's main road, then off onto a more obscure road to Gaoua in the South.

"It is a difficult journey for Europeans," he said, as he removed my bag from the taxi. I thanked Idrissa, who asked for the equivalent of ten American dollars until Bamako haggled with him in their common tongue for a minute. Then he graciously accepted five, wished me a safe journey, and sped off.

"Why did you move to Ouagadougou?" I asked Bamako.

"Work. Ouaga is the only city in Burkina where I can feed my family."

"You have many children?"

"Twelve."

"Wow."

He laughed. "That is a small African family!" The scars on his cheeks moved as he laughed, but they remained unbroken by wrinkles or creases, solid as the seams of steel soldered together. "You look at these marks on my face. You must not look at a man's face, my friend, when you are in Lobi country. You keep your eyes on the ground." Again, he squinted at me, his eyes piercing.

It occurred to me that symbols, expressions, even gestures I'd come to assume were universally synonymous with certain basic human emotions might not have the same significance here. What did it mean if you stared at someone's face or shook their hand or waved at someone? Even the guidebook had acknowledged such meanings could change from one region or ethnic group to another.

What was the meaning of those deep scars on his face? Were they symbols of an important rite of passage, or merely decorative? I had no idea what I was dealing with.

You are almost home now.

"I must go as soon as possible," I said, determined to make a move before I lost my nerve.

"Americans are always in a hurry," said Bamako without the slightest touch of amusement.

"Yes," I agreed. "What's the fastest way to get to the bus station?"

Bamako offered to take me on his moped to the *gare routière* located on the other side of town. I prayed I wouldn't be thrown from his rattling contraption as it clattered over deep potholes, darting through the obstacle course formed by other motorcycles and cars in equally precarious states, many encumbered with towers of teetering parcels.

Thankfully, the entire hub of Ouagadougou took only minutes to cross, for however important it appeared at first glance, I discovered, the city was basically a large dusty village with a few paved roads running through its center.

I had no warning we'd arrived at the bus station as there was no recognizable sign. Bamako simply shut off the engine, and I looked up to see a minivan more rusted than his moped, stacked with an impossibly giant pile of parcels, sacks, and boxes. He helped me negotiate the price of my ticket with an agent who had just emerged from a concrete block storage shed carrying a small plastic pail that looked like a child's toy watering can. The ticket was only three thousand CFA, or less than ten dollars, and the bus was due to leave in about ten minutes.

"I will keep you in my prayers, my friend," said Bamako, extending a firm handshake. "When you are in Gaoua, you will visit the museum, and they will tell you where to go for the Lobi."

Listen.

I decided I'd better use the toilet if I was going to be stuck on a crowded bus for eight hours. I asked the agent where it was, and he handed me the pail he'd just been using. It was still half-full of clear water. He pointed to the little concrete structure he'd just exited. It had no roof, just four walls, one with a doorway. Inside there was a hole in the ground the size of an ashtray.

The stink of raw sewage caused me to gag till I held my breath. Near the opening, a cluster of white maggots writhed in a tiny pool of urine. On one wall, a pair of cockroaches the size of oak leaves explored the air with their antennae. I set the pail near the entrance — apparently it was provided for washing one's hands after one finished up — and stood as close to it as possible while pissing into the hole as directly as I could manage from that distance, praying I didn't send one of the roaches in my direction.

I wasn't going to bother with the water from the pail, but then as I emerged, a woman standing over a large tub overflowing with suds and clothes shot me a suspicious look. When I poured some of the water from the pail over my left hand, rinsing it thoroughly, she bent back down over her washing. I had come from the other side of the world prepared to learn ancient secrets, but first I had to relearn the most basic fundamentals.

They will teach you.

It was all part of the journey, I realized. Everything was part of what I needed to experience to understand. When I came out, Bamako was gone, and the bus was ready to leave. Though I'd hardly gotten to know him and Idrissa, I'd at least been able to communicate with them. I felt completely and utterly alone now.

The first three or four hours of the journey on the main *autoroute* were uneventful, but I was smashed against the window by a row of well-worn travelers who traveled in complete silence. My immediate neighbor — who might just as easily have been a youthful hundred years old as a weathered forty — slept most of the way with his stifling weight pressing against my shoulder. It was just as well because, with the music blasting from the van's blown-out speakers, it was impossible to make conversation. I tried not to stare at his arm, with its series of open sores near the wrist. The smell of his stale sweat never quite evaporated, even when we picked up speed on the road. What little breeze came through the open windows was infused with the smell of kerosene and burnt leaves.

Home.

In the afternoon, we stopped for lunch near Pâ, the last town on the main road before the coach turned off to Gaoua. From what I could gather, the heart of the little village was the collection of mud huts I could see just off the road in the distance.

Women carrying large plastic tubs of food on their heads swarmed our coach. As the only white person for miles, I was a bit of a novelty to the children, who shouted "Toubaboo, Toubaboo!" and pointed at me. When I rejected their offers of red juices knotted up in plastic baggies and brown cakes balled in bits of plastic wrap, they turned away, *tsking* their disappointment to each other, and I felt a bit guilty for not buying a little something.

The scale of the poverty all around me was only beginning to hit me, I guess. Actually, I suppose I was in shock. There was the same sense of helplessness I had felt at my mother's side only days before. And now that helplessness had traveled with me to the other side of the world and extended over a continent. What would my little insights into the history of a bunch of cards do for these people who struggled each day against starvation and illness? And what would my mother do if she turned to find I wasn't there? But I had to continue now. Had to know if there was anything to be found at all.

Almost there now.

A half-hour later, we continued our trajectory, heading south. Though the main road had been little more than a crude two-lane piece of asphalt, the secondary route to Gaoua was only half that — in places littered with potholes, in others nothing more than gravel or dirt. And as we moved further from the savannah of the north into the lush vegetation of the south, the roads — washed almost completely away in places by sudden and violent rains — became increasingly difficult to navigate.

Several times, I could have sworn I heard the van's axles cracking as we crashed into deep holes. With virtually no shocks on the vehicle and no padding on the seats, it was impossible to think of anything but getting through the ordeal. From the window, I saw the occasional cluster of mud huts whoosh by. Otherwise, there was little to see but the tangle of wild vegetation we left behind in the red dust kicked up by our vehicle.

When we finally arrived in Gaoua around 8:00 p.m. — a good twelve hours after we'd begun the journey — I was famished. My fellow passengers collected their parcels from the driver, who tossed them from the roof. They'd exchanged little more than a few sentences with each other the entire route, and now they scattered in opposite directions, heading to their families with the wares they'd collected in the capital.

As my guidebook had warned me, there were only two accommodation options in town to speak of, and only one was centrally located. Luckily, there was still a vacancy at the nine-room "hotel" across from the market where the bus had dumped me. A small woman with a pink scarf wrapped around her head showed me the room. It was little more than a concrete block-box with a single rectangle of foam laid on a series of wooden slats for a bed.

The door opened directly onto the concrete porch that ran the length of the little building. Lit by a series of bare bulbs — each attracting a cacophony of strange insects — the porch led past other rooms to the communal lavatory, which consisted of a squat toilet, a large sink, and a shower with a heavily mildewed flower-print curtain. Only cold water ran from the pipes.

I asked the woman where I could get a meal. She spoke no English and only a few words of French, but we managed to communicate through a series of gestures, and I learned that for a little extra, she could fix me something herself.

I thought of my mother packing me a lunch to go to school when I was just a small child. How very far away that moment was now!

Never closer.

I unzipped my bag, which was completely covered in rusty red dust from having been strapped to the roof of the van all the way from Ouagadougou, and found my towel. But before I could head to the showers, the woman rapped on the door to my room and presented me with a bowl of "tô," or so I assumed it to be, since it fit the description of the national dish as described in my guide: a firm mass of smashed millet grains with the consistency of play dough and the color of plaster. The accompanying sauce was spicy, with leafy spinach-like vegetables and tiny red peppers. There was also a peculiar bitter flavor coming from something called "soumbala," a spice made from mashing the pods of the carob tree into little balls that looked and smelled like dried dung. I was weak from hunger, though, so I managed to get it all down.

Eating gave me a burst of energy, so I decided to check out my surroundings. I didn't make it more than a few steps from the hotel, though. A sky full of stars loomed over the vacant stands of the market. Along the streets, in darkened doorways, clusters of men huddled together, lit only by the glow of their cigarettes. Somewhere off in the distance, the tinny sounds of contemporary African music animated a dance floor, its existence betrayed by a single strand of Christmas lights sparkling at the club's entrance. Although I wouldn't have minded a drink, I couldn't imagine searching for one in those strange and dusty streets. Without daylight, I had no point of reference in this place. I had so much to learn before I could begin to truly communicate with people here. How was I going to talk to them about the subject that had drawn me here?

Just listen.

After my shower, I got into bed and tucked the mosquito net under the edges of the lumpy foam mattress, contemplating how different everything in my life had become over the few days it had taken me to get there. With my energy focused on the essentials of life — food, shelter, clean water, and sleep — I had no reason to wander off in search of mysteries. Here, every face in the crowd and every symbol in my path held a mystery for me. And the collective force of so much unknown had exactly the opposite effect on me than I'd have expected. Instead of becoming more inquisitive about each new sign, each new piece of information, my questions merged into one collective mystery that could only be explained by culture.

Yes, listen.

I woke to a rooster's crow, feeling I'd woken from a dream, yet I had no memory of one. When I discovered I couldn't shake the grogginess, however, I realized I was running a slight fever.

I'd expected as much. No matter how careful I was about eating only cooked foods, I was bound to be exposed to something. I took an icy cold shower and swallowed an aspirin, which seemed to bring down the fever, at least temporarily. I filled up an empty water bottle with tap water, purifying it with a chlorine tablet.

The woman who'd cooked me dinner was sweeping the porch outside my room. "*Petit déjeuner?*" she said as I approached.

"*Merci!*"

She dropped the broom and returned with more of the pasty tô. This time the sauce had peanut oil along with the inevitable soumbala. I got it down, somehow, in case that would be the most palatable meal available that day.

By the time I was finished, my host had finished her sweeping and was pounding millet grains with what looked like a giant mortar and pestle. She worked at a furious pace, as if unaffected by the harsh sun, which was already high and hot at 7 or 8 a.m. I opened my mouth to ask her a question, but as if sensing my presence, she anticipated my needs: *"La musée?"* she asked.

I suppose that was the same thing every one of the few weary tourists who passed through these parts had at the top of his itinerary.

"Oui," I admitted.

She dropped her pestle and motioned towards the market, which was already filling with colorful chaos.

"Marché avant," she said.

"Okay, merci."

Yes, it was too early for the museum, so first I'd tour the market. Perhaps I could find someone selling or even reading cards. After fending off dozens of men approaching me in the crowd — some offering their services as guides, others offering to show me African art, and still others simply begging for money — I finally made it into the center of the market.

From the heaps of brightly dyed fabrics to the towering piles of vegetables and grains, there wasn't an inch of the space that didn't burst with color and movement. Through it all, an open trench more than a foot wide drained rancid waste from the market's core right down the middle of the narrow dusty path that ran between vendors' overstocked stalls. Children played in the dust at the edge of this river of raw sewage, oblivious to its stench. I'd never experienced a place so alive and at the same time so precipitously on the edge of death and decay.

And nowhere in this teeming tableau of food and fabric was there a single object without a direct relationship to the essentials of life. There was food, clothing, even materials to construct shelter, but besides a few men selling African drums and statues to the rare tourists who passed through here, no one at the market sold anything even remotely extraneous, let alone Tarot cards. I was far from the privileged world of Western vanity in a land where survival was the sole reason for existence.

You are beginning to hear.

Emerging at the other side of the market, I was relieved to see a row of taxis in the distance, and I hailed the first driver who caught my eye. *"Musée? Musée?"* he sang.

"*Oui!*"

With only a few French words in his vocabulary, the driver was unable to engage me in conversation. He simply took me to a long white rectangle of a building about a mile out of the town's center on another dusty open road. The building's arched openings and slanted black roof gave it the feeling of a former colonial outpost in the jungle. As soon as we pulled up, he jumped out of the car and ran up to the entrance, pounding on the window. I heard a rattling of keys from within, and a portly man in an embroidered emerald robe emerged, rubbing the sleep from his eyes. As soon as the man's vision adjusted to the light, he welcomed me.

"*Bonjour, Monsieur.*"

"*Ah, vous parlez français!* I am Ollo. I am happy to take you on tour of our museum."

"*Merci.*"

"*Merci* to God for the French, because my English… Ohhh!" He made a gesture to the heavens as if to say even prayers wouldn't help with that. He laughed heartily, as if we'd shared an intimate joke, then turned to the driver to exchange a few words in what I presumed was Lobiri, the local language. "He will wait for you," he assured me.

Inside, the collection of artifacts was far more impressive than anything I'd imagined I'd find in such a remote region. From statuary and furnishings to weapons and tools, the collection covered every imaginable aspect of traditional Lobi culture. There were astonishing photos of ritual scarification and piercings, most of them involving the insertion of massive lip plugs of varying circumferences. There were even full-scale replicas of buildings from a typical Lobi village, including what I understood to be a ceremonial hut. Apparently, spiritual leaders inhabited such buildings, where they performed sacred rituals important to the welfare of the village. Entering the hut, I passed through an earthen labyrinth, ending up at the sacred inner chamber where light entered through a tiny hole in the ceiling. Along the way, an assortment of sacred statues and objects known as totems had been placed at strategic locations.

So close.

"When an outsider enters the space," Ollo explained, "he upsets the totems. They communicate with each other to alert the spirit world, which takes the trespasser in sacrifice. Lobi culture has remained almost perfectly preserved against outside influence," he added with an intimidating glare. I felt I was being reminded that I was very privileged indeed to be granted this peek into that sacred world and that anything I learned during my stay was to be kept in the strictest confidence.

From my guidebook I knew that the "sacrifice" he spoke of may have been attributed to the intervention of the totems, but it was actually carried out by the Lobi people themselves, who generally attacked trespassers with poisonous arrows and daggers before any questions were asked. This type of hospitality with outsiders had earned them a fierce reputation even among their neighbors in Burkina Faso.

Fascinating as it all was, though, it had little or nothing to do with the Naarem. There seemed to be no evidence of any painted barks or parchments, only statuary, and the homes in the reproduction of a Lobi village bore little or no resemblance to the homes caught in the blurry photos in Ouédrago's book.

But since Ollo seemed so delighted to have an attentive visitor, I decided to brave what I already assumed to be a fruitless question. "Have you heard of the Naarem?"

The beaming smile on his rounded face turned into a frown, and the warmth evaporated immediately from his eyes. "Who sent you?" His voice was threatening, and I thought of the strategic arrows designed to penetrate the flesh of an intruder. My fever had never completely disappeared, and I was suddenly aware of how fragile I was. I was at least a day's journey from any hospital, any embassy, any airport...

So very close.

"I'm researching the history of Tarot cards, and I found a book by someone named Ouédrago, who said he'd done his research in this area of the country." My voice was weak and trailed off. It took all my effort just to speak, let alone find the words in French.

Ollo continued to study my face, in breach of what I understood to be the African tradition of avoiding a neighbor's stare. "Ouédrago came to take our souls. He lied to us, then he lied to the world in his book."

Surely he realized that I could not have been sent directly by the author of the book.

"I had no idea. I only wanted to find the Naarem."

"The Naarem is witchcraft. It was Ouédrago who brought it here. He taught our children to paint the pictures, then he taught them to tell stories of the future. Many people died. And then he took our pictures to France to put them in a book."

"How did they die?"

"They said malaria, but it was his magic. The spirits killed him. When anyone steals the secrets of our people, he dies."

My chills multiplied as I realized this last sentence was directed at me.

"I only wanted to see for myself... I didn't know..." Perhaps my explanations were useless and by the very nature of my interest in his culture, I was considered a thief.

"The stranger never knows," he said. "It is always the same."

I was getting dizzier by the second. My head was burning. Ollo's voice echoed in my head. It was the voice of the man who had followed me in New York. The same man who had sounded so much like Salif. The voice was different from Salif's, though. I could hear the difference now. It was deeper and more threatening, and it spoke to me from outside time. I thought my brain was going to explode with the fever, and that pounding from my dream was right there in my head.

You've been waiting for this moment. Listen.

When I woke, I was being violently jostled in the passenger seat of a large jeep, which raced over potholes at alarming speeds. "You passed out," said the voice to my left. I could barely turn to see Ollo in the driver's seat. "You're going to be okay. You've been poisoned, but you will be cleansed."

"Where are we going?" I heard my voice from somewhere outside myself. I couldn't sense any movement in my lips or limbs, only a numb, icy chill. My head continued to pound. My body trembled.

"Deep into the Koulbi Forest. There is a marabout..."

"A priest? But the hospital. The embassy..."

"There is no time for that now, my friend. You were already very close to death."

"But who?"

"Rest..."

I passed out again, despite the violent bumps. I don't know how long I slept, but it was a restless sleep, full of vibrant nightmares flashed against the screen of my brain with a strobe-like frequency. The collapsing tower was not only inhabited by its usual occupants now, but with children from the streets of Ouagadougou and merchants from the Gaoua market. Raw sewage flowed through arterial gutters crawling with strange poisonous insects, as bodies scrambled in all directions trying to escape. There was Brad, Dr. Carter, Eileen, Botu, Issa, Salif… all screaming in horror as the very foundation crumbled from under them. And there were Mom and Dad, limping along, trying to hold each other up. She reached out to me, calling out for help, but the dust of the collapsing building became a thick red wall between us, and she disappeared.

I brushed against the dark, cramped walls of the tower as I floated between them. Only I realized I wasn't dreaming anymore. This wasn't the tower. These walls were real. I looked up into Ollo's face. He held me under my shoulder blades, carrying me through a labyrinth like the one at the museum, only far more elaborate. Eventually, the tunnels tapered to a dense and suffocating core.

I couldn't make out the face of the person who held my feet, but he sang some sort of repetitive, ritualistic chant as we rounded one turn of the maze after another. Finally, we emerged into the center of the structure, where the light blinded me. As my eyes adjusted, I realized I'd been left alone in a room with a man.

I couldn't tell if it was Ollo or someone else, for he wore a mask of shells and feathers. I'd been laid out on a long straw mat. I struggled to move but couldn't. The man scattered shells in the dust between us, muttered something in what was probably Lobiri, and collected them again, repeating the process.

I blacked out, only to wake moments (hours?) later to the trickle of a strong medicinal liquid between my lips. The man (a marabout?) poured the substance between my lips from a long thin gourd. When I finished drinking, I passed out again.

This went on for what could have been hours or days. I remember waking at times to the pressure of rough, warm hands on my forehead. Mostly, there were the feverish staccato images of my nightmare, mixed with the incessant chanting of the people who watched over me.

At one point, the man with the mask drew blood from my arm with a ceremonial knife. My mouth wouldn't open to scream as I felt the life draining entirely away from my system into a massive basin hollowed from a dried gourd. As I finally managed to emit a tiny scream, I awoke to find my arm unwounded and the man with the mask still whispering his steady chant beside me.

This bloodletting dream became part of my recurring nightmare now, as the colors of my visions became increasingly surreal. Images shuffled in my brain with an impossible speed. My waking and dream worlds had almost completely merged into one, and the combined landscape had no point of reference I could understand. Everything transpired in languages I didn't speak, and the faces around me, when they weren't masked, belonged to people I'd never seen before.

This was not *my* nightmare, I decided. They had put a spell on me.

And then, before I realized I'd been displaced yet again, I woke to find myself strapped back into the seat of Ollo's jeep. "Where are we..."

"You are very sick." His voice trembled. "You must go home to your family."

When I woke again, I found myself seated on a plane to Paris, with no recollection of how I'd gotten there. I went through my backpack, which, miraculously, was tucked under the seat in front of me. I'd last seen it at the hotel in Gaoua where I had left it the morning I took the taxi to the museum. Luckily, my return ticket was inside, along with my passport, though my credit cards and money were missing.

I slept most of the flight, and at Charles de Gaulle, the attendant was kind enough to take pity on my condition, escorting me to the connecting flight to New York, where the check-in agents changed my ticket to the current date, waiving the fee. I was too delirious to bother caring what day it was.

Waking just a few hours ago, we had nearly arrived in New York. I could have continued to sleep, but I needed to write all this down while I still remembered...in case I never remembered again.

Only a few moments now, until you are finally home.

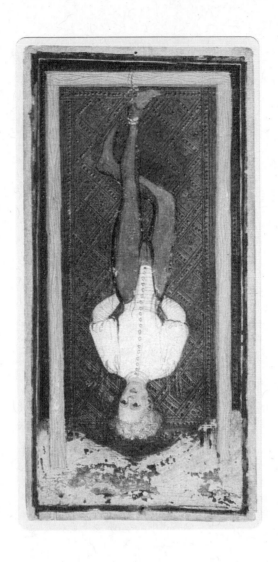

Chapter Fifteen

THE HANGED MAN

A lack of ability to help one's self through independent action. Awaiting judgment. Rebirth. The approach of new forces. Sacrifice and surrender.

The young boy with the golden curls is suspended by his left ankle from a thick rope tied to a wooden beam. His right leg is crossed behind the restrained one, and his hands are crossed behind his back where they are securely bound. Ironically, the blood rushing to the boy's cheeks gives him the same glow he would enjoy were he completely free and healthy. His shirt is buttoned tightly from the neck down to the belly, where it appears to be corseted, restricting his ability to breathe. Though the exact reason for his imprisonment unclear, it is certain the boy is entirely at the mercy of his captors.

November ?

I'm writing from my apartment now. There's a heavy pounding at the door and another in my head. I look across New York's harbor at the metallic spikes of the Manhattan skyline. Once they seemed giant and majestic. Now they are small, brittle sticks poking up against the vast horizon, shrunken by my certainty that this is the last time I will ever see them.

So little time now.

I'd thought of going directly to the emergency room from the airport, but when the plane landed, I knew it wouldn't help.

Go home.

I trudged through the slow-motion blur of faces and voices at the airport in search of an exit. The overhead speakers murmured arrival and departure information in what sounded like strange African tongues. All around me, a giant cloud of color seeped slowly through the terminals and lounges like a thick, poisonous gas. Occasionally a few cloudy streaks of pigment sharpened into focus for a moment, materializing into a face before blurring away again into the cloudy palate of colors.

At one moment, in a sudden flash of clarity, I saw Eileen standing in the distance, staring directly at me. But I lost her image in the swirl of milky images that was the crowd, and I couldn't be sure she had been real, however tangible she had seemed in that split second. Had she ever existed at all? I couldn't remember anything with any certainty anymore.

Every so often, out of my foggy peripheral vision, I caught a glimpse of the marabout who had nursed me back from the edge of death (or towards it?) in Africa. But every time I turned to find him, he was gone. The odor of the room where I lay sick for so many hours or days or weeks still seemed to permeate the air around me.

The smell of the earth you emerged from.

Somehow, I managed to put myself into a cab.

And then I was back in the crumbling building where the faceless figure pursued me around one corner after another. I ducked behind the first door that opened for me and slammed it shut, bolting it closed. Inside was a crisp hospital bed with a patient attached to a bunch of machines with long, snaking tubes. "This is my mother's room!" I protested to the trespassing patient.

"This is my room!" insisted the woman who occupied the bed. I was about to argue with her, when I noticed there was no body attached to her head, only a bloody stump wrapped in gauze and plastic. Tubes fed directly into the base of her bandaged neck, where they delivered a steady supply of bodily fluids from an assortment of bags hanging from IV stands crowding her bedside.

"Shit, they're late filling these things," she snapped, more irritated than alarmed, it seemed, that the fluids sustaining her existence were close to being exhausted. As she tried to turn towards the IV bags to size up the urgency of the situation, she slipped from the pillow and rolled off the bed, hitting the floor with a muffled thump.

As the floor gave out from under me and I fell into the billowing clouds of red dust, I knew that whoever had been pursuing me through the corridors of my nightmares had finally caught up.

Now you can rest.

I woke to find the cab driver shaking me. We had arrived at my apartment. "I was robbed. I'm sick," I said, trying to explain why I had no fare. He squealed away, shouting something about calling the police.

Inside, I hit the play button on my answering machine and collapsed on the couch. In my delirium, the dozens of voices on my machine sounded like one long steady chant or song. There were messages from Brad and Eileen asking where I'd been, interspersed with calls from credit card companies questioning charges of thousands of dollars placed on my cards in African cities I'd never even heard of.

Mixed between these voices, the frantic words of my father beat out a refrain as he pleaded with me over and over to call him. In a series of scattered messages, he told the story of my mother's deteriorating condition, the battle with doctors to stop administering painful treatments and let her die with dignity, and finally, in a sobbing conclusion, the time of her death. "Glen, where are you? If it turns out that something has happened to you as well, I... Please call."

The answering machine was still announcing the time of my father's last message when the pounding started at my door. I looked through the peephole, but it was blocked. Over the hammering, I heard an unmistakable voice bark out something in the Lobiri language, and though I still couldn't understand the meaning of the words, I understood from their intonation that I was being summoned. The voice belonged to Dad, Dr. Carter, Salif, Issa, Botu Mosabwe, Eileen, Mom...to so many of the people who had populated the last chapter of my life. And it belonged, of course, to the marabout who had hovered over me in the ceremonial building on the other side of the world.

Home.

The voice was deep and resonant. I found it comforting, somehow. And as the steady drumming on my door merged with the pounding in my head, I felt suddenly released from all pressure. The pain simply evaporated in an instant, and my thoughts grew crystal clear. There was no longer any need to worry. I didn't have much time left, only enough to capture these last moments.

But first, I pulled my Tarot cards from the outer pocket of my bag, which was still soiled with red African dirt. It no longer mattered where the cards came from or whether they contained animal or human blood. Regardless of their origin or composition, they were as alive and real as any other entity on the planet. I pulled a card from the center of the deck and turned it over, smiling as I discovered the familiar image on its surface. The Hanged Man.

Come home.

I am closing this journal once and for all as I open the door to meet the force that has come for me.

Editor's Afterword

To call Glen Harrison's death tragic would be an understatement. By compiling the young scholar's journals and notes, however, I intend not to focus attention on the tragedy of his death. Instead, I hope the presentation of his words may offer a meaningful insight into the process by which a mind may be dangerously transported by superstition. To this end, I feel Harrison's words speak for themselves, requiring little annotation.

Nevertheless, I feel I must offer some commentary on the process by which the original source materials for the present edition of Harrison's journals were chosen and edited. Aside from a few minor changes of punctuation and grammar, the first-person entries comprising the majority of the text were taken verbatim from Harrison's handwritten notes. After reading over the manuscript, Harrison's father consented to its publication, feeling, as I do, that it constitutes an important record of one individual's struggle with madness.

The descriptions of the fifteen individual Tarot cards scattered throughout the text were found paper-clipped between entries in Harrison's journal along with the corresponding cards, which were taken from Harrison's own copy of the widely available commercial reproduction of one of the earliest Italian decks, the Visconti-Sforza Tarot. Each one of these unique card descriptions was printed (presumably by Harrison) in crisp block letters on white card stock (cut to the exact proportions of cards in the Italian deck) and clipped to the card it described.

Elsewhere, Harrison's handwriting has a steady, precise structure up until his later entries, in which it becomes far more difficult to read. This shift in clarity comes at a time when the author's motor coordination had, apparently, become compromised due to his failing health. Interestingly, however, Harrison's final entry is written with the same precise structure as the earliest pages of the journal, suggesting that the author's feeling of liberation from the weakness and pain of illness, which he describes in his final poignant entry may actually have translated into a very literal — if fleeting — surge of physical strength and focus.

One of the most bizarre aspects of Harrison's journal is the inclusion of short, second-person fragments, which were squeezed into margins and between lines of text in an ostentatious cursive scrawl bearing little resemblance to Harrison's more austere everyday script. Laboratory testing of the red ink used to pen these fragments revealed traces of the late author's own blood. Throughout this manuscript, I have reproduced the cursive red fragments within the body of the main text using italics.

What led Harrison to create this omniscient voice in his journal? Madness is one obvious answer. However, having known the young man personally, I witnessed his sudden and shocking transformation from cogent, rational thinker into paranoid obsessive compulsive. I am inclined to think that Harrison's desire to experience supernatural forces — forces he wanted so desperately to believe were at work in his beloved cards — was so strong that he tried to will them into being. Not content with imagining blood smudged into the cards owned by his ancestors and painted into the first Italian Tarocchi, he seems to have attempted to tap into another dimension of consciousness by penning voices in his own blood — to a disastrous end.

In fact, the only blood found among any of Harrison's Tarot-related artifacts was his own, accounting for the smudges on what were presumably his great-grandfather's cards and on several cards in his reproduction of the Visconti-Sforza deck, including the Page of Staves. Kept with this collection was the hand-painted image of the tourist he claimed Salif had given him as well as the holy card of Saint Andrew he suspected once belonged to his great-grandfather. Harrison's association of these images with the Tarot was pure invention, as was the presence of the word "Naarem" in the completely abstract curlicues on the backs of the cards in his ancestor's deck.

The exact physical cause of Harrison's death was clarified during the autopsy. Though he'd begun taking mefloquine before his spontaneous journey to Burkina Faso, at some point during his two-week stay he failed to continue with the prophylaxis, allowing the mosquito-borne malaria parasite to infest his system.

Air Afrique personnel I contacted had only a vague recollection of Harrison, saying they remembered a quiet, disoriented young American they assumed was suffering from one of the many intestinal parasites that so commonly affect under-prepared tourists leaving Western African nations on their way back to Europe and America. None of the personnel questioned, however, thought the young man looked quite as sick as a person who had been battling full-blown malaria for days without treatment.

Medical experts I've consulted are skeptical that a Westerner with no prior exposure to malaria who became suddenly infected by the deadliest strain of the parasite known on the planet would have been able to live for more than a week without taking Fansidar or another anti-malarial antidote. However, the dates of Harrison's flights in and out of Burkina Faso were confirmed with the airline: he spent more than two weeks in the country altogether, meaning that from the time he began describing the effects of the malaria in his journal until the time he left the country amounted to more than a week: a length of time supported by the dates of the first mysterious charges on his stolen credit cards.

So just how did he survive without treating the deadly parasite? It's possible that the "marabout" who chanted over Harrison administered some sort of traditional herbal remedy against malaria that sustained the young man's fragile life for a brief time without completely curing him, though medical doctors questioned about the efficacy of herbal remedies for malaria were dismissive of any claims that such remedies had any effect on the deadly parasite. All preliminary efforts to find anyone in Gaoua and the surrounding area who remembered Harrison proved futile.

In Ouagadougou, meanwhile, the staff of the Hôtel RAN had a vague memory of the young tourist but had no recollection of him exhibiting any strange behavior during his stay.

As for the text that first drew Harrison to an interest in West Africa, *The African Origins of the Tarot* was nowhere to be found among the books left by the young scholar in his apartment at the time of his death. Nor is there any record of any such text in print, whether authored by an Abdou Ouédrago or anyone else. Indeed, the Greenwich Village bookseller who supposedly sold Harrison the book could not be found. Librarians and booksellers at many of the institutions where Harrison reports having conducted his research, however, remember communicating with the young student about the subject of his studies, the Tarot. So was the inclusion of the Ouédrago text a fictional of Harrison's tale, designed to immortalize what we might call his fictionalized thesis? Or did Harrison, in an initial fit of paranoid speculation, truly believe he had acquired such a text?

In any case, the word "Naarem" seems to be an invention of Harrison's, bearing a striking similarity to the German word for "Fool": "Der Narr." Since the character of the Fool is considered by many Tarot enthusiasts to be the principal figure of the cards — the central player who travels through the other 77 "stages of life" which they claim the cards represent — it is quite possible that Harrison invented the name for his fictional African deck based on this word.

Other incongruities in Harrison's journal were uncovered when efforts to find a Botu Mosabwe in Tottenville, Staten Island (or anywhere in five boroughs of New York) proved entirely futile.

Grace Collingsworth, meanwhile, remembered Harrison attending the training at the East Village historical museum, saying he "had a strange obsession with the occult that shifted his focus away from the history of the house, making him an unsuitable candidate for docent." When questioned about the existence of playing cards, Tarot decks or "Nared" at the museum, Collingsworth said that aside from one 19th-century deck of playing cards, the museum housed nothing of the sort in its collection. When the museum's single deck of cards was examined, no missing corners were discovered.

As for Eileen, it seems she'd called in "completely frazzled" one day to announce she wouldn't be coming back to the museum, saying she was leaving New York at once to return to her family, though no one who knew her from the museum was sure where her family lived.

Carl French, the manager at Bistro Bordeaux, said Glen was a bit "new agey" but did well enough as a server once he became familiar with the restaurant's routine. Regarding Issa and Salif, he couldn't be sure exactly what had happened to them, though he'd heard they had left the country. As for whether or not they were deported, he claimed that they had presented him with all the necessary paperwork for legal employment in his restaurant and declined to comment further.

With respect to Brad Slater, who also worked at the restaurant, Mr. French said only that he failed to show up for work one day and never came in again. Having worked with the young man at the university myself, I'd had a similar experience. Shortly after recovering from my heart attack, I learned that Brad hadn't shown up to the university for weeks. During my absence, the university had attempted to contact him and then his family and finally New York City police. It seems he had been arrested in a sting on a major marijuana grow-op functioning under the guise of a funeral parlor in the East Village. The owner of the operation, a Burkina Faso national, was arrested, and several of the illegal immigrants working for him were deported to West Africa. Though the police couldn't confirm the names of the deportees, they were able to confirm that Brad had been the "face" of the operation, supplying dealers across the five boroughs with a supply of marijuana, though it was the team's involvement in trafficking prescription opiates that landed Slater a long prison sentence.

Though Slater had often seemed a bit high-strung, I had absolutely no idea the young man had been involved in anything illicit and was quite stunned by the revelation. Given Glen Harrison's tendency to invent paranoid scenarios of mystical significance, it's not hard to see how he was able to transform the suspicious behavior he observed in Brad into something even more sinister.

Now, for entirely selfish reasons, the portrait in Glen's journal that I found most disturbing was the one of myself. In preparing this manuscript for publication, I had to swallow my pride and restrain myself from editing some of the author's most unflattering descriptions of me. After all, his criticism of me is not entirely unfounded, and the stinging truth of his words has caused me to reexamine my entire career. That I have allowed myself to sit too comfortably in the knowledge that my earlier studies were conclusive is an unfortunate mistake for which I take full responsibility. Since reading Harrison's journal, I have begun to make every possible effort to stay abreast of latest trends and new methodologies in order to not allow myself to stagnate intellectually, as indeed, I had grown accustomed to do.

Despite these painful truths, Harrison's belief that his subject matter was somehow of no interest to me because it had become associated with the occult during the 18th and 19th centuries could not have been further from the truth. From the moment the young student presented his topic, I was intrigued by the opportunity it presented for the discovery of a rather obscure body of artwork. Knowing little about the subject myself, I merely awaited his presentation to discover the Tarot for myself. Unfortunately, his obsession with the Tarot's mystical associations tore him away from an in-depth study of the cards' secular origins and made it difficult for me to relate to his interests in an academic context.

In fact, the journal gives me too much credit for being open minded about many of his wildest notions: though I told Glen I would consider contacting my colleague at the Morgan Library about the card from Bergamo that had supposedly made a surprise appearance in New York, I never actually followed up. Seeing the stress that his mother's illness was causing him, I wanted merely to erase any concerns that could have prevented him from attending to his familial obligations, so I made a vague promise that I never seriously intended to keep. Perhaps this was irresponsible on my part, but it seemed the best way I could be helpful to the troubled young man at the time.

Naturally, had I known the full extent of his distress, I may have considered a different course of action. But hindsight is hardly useful, particularly after an untimely death has occurred. In any case, I was battling my own demons at the time. Only after recovering from my heart attack was I able to take inventory of my life and adjust my priorities. Had Harrison approached me at this more reflective stage of my career, perhaps I could have been more helpful to him, but at that moment I was as blind to his situation as I was to my own.

As for the message Harrison claims I left on his machine saying the card from Bergamo had simply disappeared, this was another of his creative fabrications, created perhaps out of a desire for easy answers or possibly out of his own madness. The message I delivered to Glen while recovering in the hospital, however, was entirely true. I did ask him to forgive me for underestimating the importance of his research. My only regret was not sending that message before it was too late.

In an interesting side note, while preparing this manuscript for publication I did contact Barry Levi, a colleague at the Morgan Library, and I learned that the Page of Staves from Bergamo had never been sent to New York, at least not to the knowledge of anyone at the library.

Even stranger, around the time of Harrison's death, a G. Wittkop telephoned the library for help with orchestrating the loan of a card from the Visconti-Sforza deck for inclusion in a major exhibition on the history of the Tarot in Connecticut. Records show the individual was informed of the library's strict policy of never loaning the cards outside the library. To the best of anyone's knowledge, the exhibition never took place. The card this mysterious collector requested was the Hanged Man.

Glen's untimely death has caused me to spend many a sleepless night pondering the boundaries between fact and fiction, academia and mysticism, proof and belief. Were my interpretations of these boundaries too rigid, and could my failure to listen have contributed to his paranoia and his eventual demise? I'm afraid I'll never have a definitive answer.

Sadly, the most tragic chapter of Glen Harrison's story proved to be the most true to life. In a tearful interview, Harrison's father verified the details of his wife's cancer and subsequent death. During the final stages of her illness, while Glen was in West Africa, Mr. Harrison had no idea of his son's whereabouts until he received the fateful call from the hospital in New York which told him his son had been found dead by police when they came to his door after receiving a complaint from a cab driver about an unpaid fare.

We will never know for sure if the younger Harrison suffered from a sudden bout of mental illness brought about by his inability to face such realities as his uncertain future in academia or the inevitability of his mother's death, or whether his paranoid delusions were the direct product of the superstitious belief in the divinatory qualities of the Tarot revealed in these pages.

More ominous, perhaps, is the idea that Harrison may have deliberately orchestrated his demise to fit into the plot of the novel his journal/thesis had become. If the latter scenario seems a stretch of the imagination, consider these final notes scribbled in Harrison's own blood in the ornate script of his omniscient narrator on the back of his journal:

Divination: Communication with the divine. Seeing from a "divine" view. Ritual communication with the unconscious. The magical act of discovering the unknown.

Divine comes from the Latin *divinus*, meaning "of a god." In Hebrew, Y (Yod) represents Deity as Father; H (Heh) represents Deity as Mother. Yod-Heh is also the number fifteen.

To divine: To conjecture, guess, or make out by supernatural insight. (Most statements made by ancient oracles were not predictions but advice on how to keep the favor of the divine.)

In studying the Tarot and writing in his journal, was Glen Harrison merely playing god? It's a thought that should serve to humble anyone who has gone to great lengths to create anything. However informed we may think our own creative imaginations, as mere humans we are all too capable of letting them run straight into madness.

Towards the end of his life, Harrison's waking reality merged more and more closely with his dream world. It was as if he believed the end of the world was literally upon him, and that the contemporary world as he knew it was literally about to collapse. By believing this, he made it so.

Fortunately, unlike the collapsing building in Glen's unstable mind, the pillars of our contemporary civilization are grounded in rational thought. But if we allow fear to erode the very foundation of our world, our entire identity can crumble in an instant, imprisoning us in our own belief.

Dr. Elliott Carter, September 7, 2001

Publisher's Afterword

There have been few events in my long career as a publisher as shocking as the collapse of the Twin Towers in New York City on September 11, 2001. Along with the rest of the world, I watched in horror as the events of that dark day unfolded. For me, having received the edited journals of Glen Harrison from Dr. Carter only days before, the tragedy held a particularly ominous significance.

I attempted to call the professor numerous times to discuss his interpretation of the grim events and their relationship to the manuscript of his late student, but he returned neither phone nor email messages.

Weeks later, I learned from his family that on the morning of September 11, Dr. Carter had been on his way to a meeting at the World Trade Center. His family was uncertain of the details of the fateful encounter, only that it had something to do with "rare Italian artifacts" and that the professor was quite excited about the engagement, though he wished to keep the details secret from even them and his colleagues.

Finding not a single trace of their loved one in the years following the tragedy, the Carter family finally accepted his disappearance as definitive proof of his death in the towers' collapse.

For nearly a decade, I hesitated to publish the Harrison manuscript, fearing that the association of its contents with September 11 would be misinterpreted as opportunistic, or worse, that it would have the very effect that its editor, Dr. Carter, wished to avoid: fueling fear with superstition.

Ultimately, however, I decided that it is not the job of a publisher to interpret a piece of writing but to present it in the sharpest light, providing the best conditions for allowing readers to interpret it for themselves.

Nevertheless, in preparing the manuscript for publication, I assigned a new editor to the project in Spring of 2010 to fact-check some of the claims made in Dr. Carter's afterword. The editor was unable to locate anyone at the Morgan Library who recalled being contacted by Dr. Carter, but then it turned out that one — and only one — employee of the Morgan Library had also disappeared on

September 11, 2001: Barry Levi. When Levi's Outlook calendar was searched for clues about his disappearance, it turned out he'd been on his way to the World Trade Center. It was assumed that he was among those who perished in the tragedy that day. On his calendar the following note was discovered:

"Mr. Weydraygan, Griot Press, World Trade Center."

No evidence of the existence of such a press in either tower could be found anywhere.

Even without that last chilling detail, I find it impossible to read the pages of Harrison's journal without being haunted by the timing of the events that immediately followed their composition. Were Harrison's seemingly mad insights a mere coincidence, or were they actually a foreshadowing of world events communicated to him in a strange mystical language not capable of translation into rational thought? I leave it for readers to decide.

Marcus Odin, September 11, 2011

About the Author

Born in Chicago, Don Bapst has lived in New York, San Francisco, London, Paris, Ouagadougou, Montreal, Toronto, and Los Angeles. He holds a Master of Fine Arts in Creative Writing from Brooklyn College, where he studied with Allen Ginsberg, and his work has been published in numerous anthologies and magazines including *Exquisite Corpse, The Columbia Poetry Review, Evergreen Chronicles,* and *blue magazine*. A French translation of his novel *danger@ liaisons.com* was published in 2010 by Éditions Popfiction in Montreal, and his theatrical work has been staged in Chicago, New York, Montreal, and Toronto. Also a filmmaker, Bapst's short films have been screened in Toronto, Montreal, and Cannes. He has also translated two novels and a collection of short stories into English from the French, including Gabrielle Wittkop's *Necrophiliac* (ECW, 2011).